T0077371

Ju|'hoan Folktales:
Transcriptions and English Translations

*A Literacy Primer by and for
Youth and Adults of the Ju|'hoan Community*

Edited by   Megan Biesele

|Ai!ae Fridrick |Kunta	Tsamkxao Fanni |Ui
Beesa Crystal Boo	|Ui Charlie N!aici
Dabe Kaqece	|Asa N!a'an
Dam Botes Debe	Dahm Ti N!a'an
Di||xao Cgun	Di||xao Pari |Kai
G‡kao Martin |Kaece	N!ani |'Kun
Hacky Kgami Gcao	!Unn|obe Morethlwa
Jafet Gcao Nqeni	||Ukxa N!a'an
Kaqece Kallie N!ani	|Xoan N!a'an
|Koce |Ui	Catherine Collett
Polina Riem	Taesun Moon

Order this book online at www.trafford.com
or email orders@trafford.com

Most Trafford titles are also available at major online book retailers.

© Copyright 2009 Kalahari People's Fund.
All rights reserved. No part of this publication may be reproduced, stored in a retrieval system, or transmitted, in any form or by
any means, electronic, mechanical, photocopying, recording, or otherwise, without the written prior permission of the author.

Print information available on the last page.

ISBN: 978-1-4269-9809-6 (sc)

Because of the dynamic nature of the Internet, any web addresses or links contained in this book may have changed
since publication and may no longer be valid. The views expressed in this work are solely those of the author and do
not necessarily reflect the views of the publisher, and the publisher hereby disclaims any responsibility for them.

Any people depicted in stock imagery provided by Getty Images are models, and
such images are being used for illustrative purposes only.
Certain stock imagery © Getty Images.

Trafford rev. 02/09/2021

Trafford PUBLISHING® www.trafford.com

North America & international
toll-free: 844-688-6899 (USA & Canada)
fax: 812 355 4082

We dedicate our work to the late \Ai!ae Benjamin \Aice and Ghau G\aq'o, translators and transcribers, who died in 2008 while we were working on this book.

Contents

Introduction

The Concept and Format of this Book

This Juǀ'hoan-language literacy primer has been produced by the Juǀ'hoan Transcription Group, active since 2002 in Nyae Nyae, Namibia. The members of the Transcription Group, all Juǀ'hoan men and women, used first ExpressScribe and then ELAN transcription software, and digitized versions of Juǀ'hoan folktales recorded in Botswana and Namibia between 1971 and 2006, to prepare the selections for the primer. Meant as literacy study materials for youth and adults of the Juǀ'hoan communities of both countries, the fourteen selected tales are arranged in order of increasing length and complexity. The tales are not compilations from various versions, but faithful renderings of specific recordings. They are accompanied by both literal, line-by-line English translations and short English synopses.

At the beginning of each tale is provided a summary, the name of the raconteur, the place and date of the recording, and the names of the people involved in its transcription and translation. The text itself is in an interlinearized format where Juǀ'hoan transcriptions and corresponding English translations are given on alternating lines. The Juǀ'hoan text is in roman (i.e. unvarnished) type and the English text is in italic type. Every other line of the Juǀ'hoan has been numbered to facilitate searching and indexing for students. Line breaks in the transcriptions directly reflect the pauses made by the raconteur and, at least for native speakers of the language, make for a more natural reading experience. Occasional questions and terms of direct address interspersed in the text reflect the presence of the interviewer and have been retained for authenticity.

A few of the written names of the Juǀ'hoan people involved in the preparation of this book utilize an orthographic system that is distinct from the standard orthography adopted by the community and the Namibian government [1]. These names are written according to the practice in Botswana and use roman letters for click symbols. In such names, *c* corresponds to ǀ and *q* to ǃ. This is a direct consequence of the diversity of the people involved in the project.

The Kalahari Peoples Fund (KPF), a US nonprofit that has been active in sup-

---

[1] Patrick Dickens, "Juǀ'hoan Orthography in Practice," *S. Afr. Tydskr. Afrikatale* 11/1 (1991).

port of San community initiatives in southern Africa since the 1970s, has been a major source of both financial and volunteer support to this primer. During the apartheid-era 1980s, the Namibian Ju|'hoan community, to whom schooling was available only in Afrikaans, asked KPF for "real" schoolbooks in their language. KPF has helped to provide this book to enrich the small but growing body of educational materials available in the Ju|'hoan language. Because it is as authoritatively prepared as possible, using the Dickens English-Ju|'hoan, Ju|'hoan-English Dictionary [2] adopted by the Ju|'hoan community and the Government of the Republic of Namibia, the book can also be used by linguists and other scholars, and by the general public interested in Ju|'hoan San culture. The project has been authorized by the Education Committee of the Nyae Nyae Conservancy as well as by members of the Ju|'hoan Curriculum Committee, several of whom have worked as teachers in the Nyae Nyae Village Schools Project and are also part of the Transcription Group.

The Transcription Group members were trained in computer literacy and transcription skills by Catherine Collett and Taesun Moon, technical assistants to Megan Biesele, who facilitated the book project. Taesun Moon also typeset this book in LaTeX. Dr. Biesele, an anthropologist/community facilitator who has worked with Ju|'hoan communities since 1970, made the recordings on which this book is based. Fluent in the Ju|'hoan language, she worked closely with the storytellers and the Ju|'hoan transcribers on each of the texts. The Transcription Group decided to undertake translation into English as well, for three main reasons: 1) English is an official language of both Namibia and Botswana, 2) English literacy is desired by both communities for economic reasons in addition to Ju|'hoan literacy, and 3) translations will make the Ju|'hoan tales accessible to a wide world of interested readers in other countries, as well.

The Trafford First Voices Publishing Programme has generously made possible the publication of this primer, and its first 40 copies will be distributed free to the community. The primer is an addition to several other heritage and curriculum materials that have been locally produced for the community's schools over the years. Since community access is the central focus of the project, it is commendable that Trafford has also agreed to the primer's simultaneous publication on the World Wide Web, at www.kalaharipeoples.org/texts. This means that the online version can be instantly updated if viewers find corrections that need to be made, or want to suggest different interpretations or translations. This form of publication is attuned both to the traditionally collaborative learning style of the Ju|'hoan people and to the spirit of the Internet today, where relevant communities and knowledgeable individuals work together, via Wiki technology, to create and constantly update bodies of shared information.

---

[2]Patrick Dickens, *English-Ju|'hoan Ju|'hoan-English Dictionary* (Cologne: Rüdiger Köppe Verlag, 1994).

The History of the Transcription Project

The Kalahari Peoples Fund, run with the volunteer labor of professional anthropologists, educators, and writers, has been involved in many phases of background work to make this project possible. These phases include community consultation and development in liaison with the Ju|'hoan people's organization; the founding of an alternative mother-tongue school project; the development of an orthography[3], grammar[4], dictionary[5], and teaching materials in the Ju|'hoan language; the training of computer-literate Ju|'hoan teachers; and the training of young Ju|'hoan people in linguistic techniques and the use of ELAN, the discipline standard transcription software developed at the Max Planck Institute of Psycholinguistics, Nijmegen, The Netherlands.

In southern Africa now as in much of the world, many indigenous people like the Ju|'hoan and other San take an active role in educational projects for their young people. Closely associated with many of these projects are efforts in cultural heritage preservation and local language development. In some cases NGOs as well as anthropologists and linguists have become part of educational support teams to provide professional training to local teachers as well as to community members concerned with heritage and language development.

Many groups of San are also acknowledging the importance of mother-tongue education for at least the first three years of school. These groups value developing skills of critical thinking as well as promoting retention of endangered languages and heritage. Following consensus of most international educational experience, the trend among San educational projects is to insist on mother-tongue instruction for 3-4 years until the basic skills of literacy are gained, at which point those skills can be generalized for use in whatever national language may be most useful, such as English.

One such project has been going on among the Nyae Nyae Ju|'hoan San of Namibia for nearly twenty years. Since Namibian Independence in 1990, an imaginative and comprehensive Village Schools Project (VSP) has provided a matrix for the creation of a broad range of local-language curriculum and enrichment materials. There has been a large participation of community members of all ages in the production of materials. The VSP has also tried to honor the very effective means of learning and child socialization long practiced by the Ju|'hoansi and other San. San societies put a high valuation on equality and sharing, and in the VSP their children's learning has taken place in a hands-on, informal, narrative- and experience-rich environment, involving children of all ages with local teachers and many adults.

The experience of the Village Schools Project has been instrumental in convinc-

---

[3]Dickens *Orthography, op. cit.*
[4]Patrick Dickens, *A Concise Grammar of Ju|'hoan* (Cologne: Rüdiger Köppe Verlag, 2005).
[5]Dickens *Dictionary, op. cit.*

ing some Namibian educational authorities to honor the egalitarian values of the Ju|'hoansi. Among some participants, as well, there has been the realization that genuinely creative literature and non-fiction learning materials must be provided for readers beyond the first few years, to enable an actual literate tradition to develop.

The local Ju|'hoan language committee has worked with linguists coordinated by the Kalahari Peoples Fund to provide a user-friendly orthography of their phonetically-complex language. Computer literacy and digital media are gradually becoming available to the Ju|'hoan educational project, where technological empowerment has quickly increased political effectiveness for the surrounding communities.

Since 2002, digital tape-recorders and videocams have been used by Ju|'hoan trainees and Village Schools students to gather local information from older members of their communities. Some of the elders are respected healers, and they contributed narratives of psychic healing using altered states of consciousness and laying on of hands. Others are community leaders, and they recorded their memories and perspectives on the exciting political process by which they became citizens of a modern nation state after Namibia's struggle for Independence. Products have included contributions to two existing interactive websites, www.kalaharipeoples.org and www.kalaharipeoples.net, several books and other publications, as well as desktop-published informal curriculum.

In preparation to create this book, Village Schools Project teachers and Curriculum Committee members have been in training since 2002. They learned computer literacy, translation, and other linguistic techniques with Megan Biesele, KPF's Director; with linguist Tom Gueldemann of Leipzig and Zurich; and with KPF's webmasters and technical assistants, Catherine Collett, Taesun Moon, and Lesley Beake. Laptop computers were donated to the community via KPF by Sony in the United States and by the Redbush Tea Company in London, and solar panels to run them were donated by British Petroleum.

By June, 2006, however, solar was no longer necessary. The project was able to make use of the new, Norwegian-funded Captain Kxao Kxami Community Learning and Development Centre, complete with electricity, in the administrative centre, Tsumkwe. Now, 3 to 7 Ju|'hoan trainees have been working 9-to-5 days on the laptops, producing hundreds of pages of authentic Ju|'hoan story texts from digital soundfiles. As news of the project has grown in the community, and people old and young came to see what was going on, the trainees have been able to workshop some of the texts with the very storytellers who told the stories in the first place. It has been an exhilarating time of group learning and productivity, with roots going back to the creative early days of the Village Schools Project.

The Transcription Group has spun off two new projects of its own, as well. In 2007 the transcribers decided to add a Youth Transcription component so they could pass on their new skills to younger Ju|'hoan people, especially girls, who have very little access to employment. Second, additions to the current Jul'hoan Dictionary are emerging from the transcriptions, and since 2008 a Jul'hoan manager has been working with the transcribers and with linguist Amanda Miller to professionally update the Dictionary.

A guiding principle in all this language development work is the Jul'hoan people's empowerment to tell their own stories. A further guiding principle is integration with the school curriculum of the Village Schools Project, which has now become part of the national school system of Namibia. Last, the projects emphasize respect both for ancient lifeways and for contemporary creativity. They are conservation-oriented, foster moral ownership of the creative process by Jul'hoan people themselves, and creatively use information technology. Based on sound research and full community participation, they foster educational and documentation measures to protect the Jul'hoan culture, to produce both curriculum and archives for the Jul'hoan community, and to provide publications for scholars and others via the World Wide Web.

Related Websites and the Future

Previous projects involving the Kalahari Peoples Fund and making the present one possible included construction of a high-speed internet connection during 2006 - 2008 at Tsumkwe, the remote Jul'hoan administrative center in northeastern Namibia where the project is based, for exchange of transcribed and edited texts along the road to publication. The internet connection has additionally made it possible for Jul'hoan San students to establish an email exchange with young people in the US and other parts of the world.

In July, 2008, KPF launched its new southern African website, www.kalaharipeoples.net, based in Cape Town, in two workshops in Namibia. In Windhoek, the capital, the launch took place at TUCSIN, The University Center for Studies in Namibia, with the participation of WIMSA, the Working Group of Indigenous Minorities in Southern Africa. In Tsumkwe, a remote administrative center in the northeast part of the country, it took place at the Captain Kxao Kxami Community Learning and Development Centre, with the participation of San Education Project officials from the Namibia Association of Norway; with Kalahari Peoples Fund officers and volunteers, with officers of the Nyae Nyae Conservancy, the local people's organization; and many members of the Nyae Nyae Jul'hoan San community.

Participants included a spectrum of Jul'hoan people, from the most educated to many who are non-literate. One of the most eloquent speeches in favor of the new website was made by an elderly woman storyteller who has worked with the Transcription Group and who was glad her recorded stories could appear on the website in audio and video form. Others drew attention to some of the creative writing of local people-in both the Juǀʼhoan language and English-on the site (See "My Girlfriend and the Dictionary" under "Cultural" and "Stories" at www.kalaharipeoples.net for an example!)

KPF had been considering for some time the idea of a network that would link the widely spread communities of San people and the organizations that work most closely with them. In addition, KPF saw a need for a link that would provide information to the many people worldwide who request information about the San peoples and express interest. The KPN website fulfills both these needs, and provides a forum as well for the exciting new practice of Digital Storytelling work-shops that is empowering nonliterate communities on several continents.

Along with KPN, the Kalahari Peoples Fund also continues to maintain and upgrade its original US-based website, www.kalaharipeoples.org. The new www.kalaharipeoples.net links San communities and organizations and provide a way for San people to publicize their heritage, to launch new writing and vi-sual arts initiatives, and to inform the wider world about their culture. The ex-isting KPF website, www.kalaharipeoples.org, provides human rights updates and academic and linguistic information. In November, 2008, for instance, tran-scriptions and translations of Juǀʼhoan oral literature began to become available at www.kalaharipeoples.org/texts. KPF has provided the KPN site itself, and the temporary services of a manager/editor to channel submissions and keep the site lively and active - something all website proprietors soon find to be the most time-consuming task of all. Training is being provided so that the site can be managed in future by San people themselves. Meanwhile, all the San community and orga-nizational websites wishing to participate are linking up and beginning to refer to each other, providing a solid information base on the worldwide web.

Acknowledgments

Megan Biesele, technical assistants Catherine Collett and Taesun Moon, and the Juǀʼhoan Transcription Group have many people to thank for help in making this book possible. First, it would not exist without for the Juǀʼhoan men and women storytellers of Botswana and Namibia who so enthusiastically shared their sto-ries and knowledge. Next we acknowledge all those who helped put together and carry out the Village Schools Project, from the late linguist Patrick Dickens in the 1980s to the current Principal, Cwisa Cwi. We include in the large number of those who made the VSP possible Melissa Heckler, Magdalena Broermann, and Lesley Beake. We thank SIDA, the Swedish International Development Agency, and the Embassy of Sweden in Namibia, particularly Sten Rylander and Ingrid Lofstrom-Berg, for financial and moral support to the VSP that has enabled many of the educational and heritage-preservation activities leading to the Transcription Project.

We thank Trine Strom Larsen and Jenny Beate Moller, Coordinators of the San Education Project of the Namibia Association of Norway, and we thank Wilbard Kudumo, CLDC Director, for making it possible for the Transcription Group's activities to be housed at the Community Learning and Development Centre (CLDC) in Tsumkwe. We thank the Texas Chapter of the Explorers' Club for funding a major addition, under construction in 2009, to the CLDC's library, a seminar room where transcription can be carried out in such a way as not to interfere with other library activities.

We are grateful for the steady support of the Nyae Nyae Conservancy (NNC) and its predecessor organizations through the years, and thank especially Tsamkxao ǂOma, its first Chairman, and ǀ'Angnǃao ǀ'Un, its second Chairman and head of the NNC Education Committee. We thank the staff of the Nyae Nyae Development Foundation of Namibia, the Namibian NGO that has provided support to the NNC. We thank the Kalahari Peoples Fund, the US nonprofit which has raised funds to support the Transcription Group. Major funding was provided to KPF for this project by The Redbush Tea Company of London (www.redbushtea.com). We thank the Firebird Foundation for Anthropological Research, Phillips, Maine, USA, and the Jutta Vogel Foundation of Cologne, Germany, for donating funds to KPF to support the transcription trainees' work. Our sincere thanks to Trafford Publishing for generously donating the publishing costs of this book. Thanks also to FirstVoices.com, and especially to Pauline Edwards, for their initiation and stewardship of the Trafford FirstVoices Publishing Program. We also thank several anonymous US and European donors and donor organizations–you know who you are!–for ancillary project funds.

Acknowledgments are due to German linguists Tom Gueldemann and Hans Boas, Namibian linguists Wilfrid Haacke and Levi Namaseb, and US linguists Tony Woodbury, Bonny Sands and Amanda Miller for their valuable professional consultation, participation, and advice. We thank the University of Texas Liberal Arts Information Technology Services for digitization of the entire Juǀ'hoan text collection. Last, Megan Biesele acknowledges the indispensable financial and moral support of her husband, Steve Barclay, her late father, Dr. John J. Biesele, and her sister, Jane Hinchliffe, along with the US National Institute of Mental Health, the US National Science Foundation, the US National Endowment for the Humanities, and the Wenner-Gren Foundation for Anthropological Research in funding her Botswana and Namibia research trips and text processing activities over many years.

Chapter 1

The Moon Dies and Lives Again

SUMMARY.   This story describes the waning of the moon as a death, and its re-growth as the promise of eternally renewed life.

SPEAKER.   *‖Ukxa N!a'an*

RECORDED.   Dobe, Botswana, 1971

TRANSCRIBED BY.   *|Ai!ae Fridrick |Kunta, Jafet Gcao Nqeni, Tsamkxao Fanni |Ui*

ka ha ka ku du ‖'aka
then he did and then
!ai ‖'aka ha n|a
² *died and then he certainly*
to'a te ha ku ce g!a din n!ang
went over there and then he again went back
ce g!a khuinto'a
⁴ *again went back to that same place over there*
ka ka o g|u !om
and it was the middle of the night
ka khoe ka o djo
⁶ *it was like it was black*
ka ha g!a ha ha
when he went back he he
ha ge ge ka |am ku
⁸ *he stayed and stayed and then the sun*
n‡hao ka g!a ku g|ai
went down and then he went back and came out

1

okaa kahin ha ka o n!ui n!a'an
then therefore he became the big moon

o ka kahin ha ku ha g!a ku g|aia khuinto'a
it was that he had gone back to come out at that same place over there

ǁ'a ju sa ko "uuh, a goaq ku n‡oahn,"
and the people said "ooh, you long ago told us,"

ha n!uia goaqha ku n‡oahn, o |'an ha ka !ai
the moon had long ago told them, that he would die

ka ka ha, ha koah
then then he, he shortly afterwards

o ka ha ku ku ha
it was that he was going to

'in
yes

du |'an ha ka !ai ǁ'an kahin ha ku ce g!a din n!ang ka
die and therefore he again went back over there and

ko ko ka kua !ai
did that and soon died

kua !ai
soon died

ee
yes

Chapter 2

The Honey and the Flies

SUMMARY.   When the god G!ara was still on the earth, he wanted to imitate the cardinal woodpecker by chopping out honey from a hive high in a tree. But he did not have the whistling magic or the ability to fly possessed by the woodpecker, so he fell to the ground and his stomach burst. Flies came and sewed up his stomach, and G!ara thanked the flies.

SPEAKER.   *Dahm Ti N!a'an*

RECORDED.   Kauri, Botswana, 1971

TRANSCRIBED BY.   *|Ui Charlie N!aici, G‡kao Martin |Kaece*

haa
he
‖'aixa n!a'an
the god
²
‖'aixa n!a'an
the god
he ju ko ha te o G!ara, ha hin tsi g‖xun n!ore
⁴
people say that he is G!ara, the one who created the earth
te ha !'aun!'aun
and the cardinal woodpecker
ku ‖xan cu zo
⁶
was looking around for honey
‖xan cu zo te ha !'aun!'aun tsi ho zo te-u ‖ohm
he was looking around for honey and the cardinal woodpecker found the honey and was chopping it

ku ǁohm hi te ha tsi gǀae nǀang

8

was chopping then he (G!ara) came and sat down

te nǀang te ku g≠araa ha ko hi

he sat and asked him for it

te ha ǁohm hi, ǁohm hi, ǁohm hi, ǁohm hi, ǁohm hi te ǁauhn

10

and he chopped it, chopped it, chopped it, chopped it, chopped it and whistled

ǁauhn ha tcisa ha !aro, ke sin tan-ǀ'osi

he whistled up the things he was carrying on a pole, and flat dishes

te ka !'aan te ha ≠'haan hi ko ǁ'akoa

12

they flew up to him and he put the honey in them

≠'han hi,≠'han hi te ǁ'oana hi !aroa te tsaua ha te gǀae u

put it in them, put it in them and put the carrying pole of honey over his shoulder and left him and went off

te ǁa'i nǀui cete

14

and one day again

ha G!ara cete u

G!ara again went

te tsi gǀae ho hi te-u ǁohm

16

and he came and found it and was chopping it

te ha !'aun!'aun tsi gǀae nǀang

and the cardinal woodpecker came and sat down

ee, ha ǁohm hi, ǁohm hi, ǁohm hi

18

yes, he chopped it, chopped it, chopped it

te ko ha ni ≠oa, ko ha ni ≠oa tca !'aun!'aun goaq oo, nǀang

and he tried to imitate, tried to imitate what the woodpecker had done, but

ǁauhn tama tcisi te ko ka !'an nǀang ha ǁ'oana hi u

20

failed to whistle up the things so they would come up to him so that he could carry them on his shoulders and leave

te ka !xau te sin nǀhuia ha ǀkaisi ko ka te

but they refused so he just climbed down the tree and

te tsi ≠xuru te !'an ≠'han hi

22

and then climbed back up and went and put it in

te ǁ'oanaa ǁ'akoa

and put it over his shoulder there

te ko ha ni ku tsau te ǁxoaǁxoaraa ǁ'akoa te tsi ≠aeh te ha gǀu !hara

24

and tried to fly but fell down and when he hit the ground, his stomach burst

ha !'aun!'aun tsi ≠aeh nǀhui hi tciasi te !auh

the cardinal woodpecker came and took the honey things and left

ee, mama

26

yes, mother

te ha gǀu !hara te ha sin cu te

and his stomach split and he just lay there and

si!a tsi ǂaeh ǁkaea ha

28 *they all came and gathered around him*

te ku nǂom ha g!u te ku nǂom ha g!u

and worked on his stomach and worked on his stomach

te si!a !xare tsi ǂaeh sin n!ai ka ha tjin

30 *and others came and just bit him until he cried*

a re ca !'han zoaqzoaq wa?

do you know flies?

ee,mama, tcimhsa to'a tzeamh he o zoaqzoaq

32 *yes, mother, those little things here that are flies*

ǁ'a zoaqzoaq tsi gǀae

those flies came

gǀae gǁxun ha g!au san to'a ha khoetca n!un ka 'inhin

34 *lay his hands there as if standing and doing like this*

tzanǂhao te ku g!ai ha

concentrated on sewing his

tchinǀho te g!ai, g!ai, g!ai te g!ai ǁkae te ha ui ha te ko: "Ee, mi tsuma gu mi"

36 *midriff and sewed, sewed, sewed and sewed it together and he thanked him and said "Yes, my nephew, take me up"*

ha koe tsau kxui , ee

that's how he got up, yes

mama ee

38 *mother, yes*

tca sa koh du tsi to'a

that's how they have been doing things

40

Chapter 3

A Woman First Found Fire

SUMMARY. The first person to find fire was a woman. She sat by the fire and fed her children cooked food, while her husband slept in the dark and ate raw food. After waiting a long time, the husband stole the fire and ran off, and since then fire has been known throughout the world. It was a woman who first found fire because "a woman naturally is a great thing."

SPEAKER. |Asa N!a'an

RECORDED. Kauri, Botswana, 1971

TRANSCRIBED BY. Hacky Kgami Gcao, |Ai!ae Fridrik |Kunta, G‡kao Martin |Kaece

    jua kxaice ho da'a
    the first person to find fire
    o dshau
2   *was a woman*
    dshaua hin tsi kxaina ho da'a
    that woman who first found fire
    a tsa'a
4   *you hear*
    mi ‡xae
    my daughter
    ha hin tsi kxaice ho da'a
6   *this person first found fire*
    te tcihinto'a a txun goaq n‖ae !oa kxuia a
    that is what your grandmother long ago told you

ǁ'akaa ha tse ǁae ha
then she went on and kept her

8

ǁae ha mhsi te siǃa ku 'ma ya da'a
kept her children and they all ate at the fire

te ha ǃ'hoan ku tzaa gǀu nǃang
but her husband slept in the dark

10

koara da'a te
had no fire and

koara da'a te tse ku tzaa gǀu nǃang
had no fire and then slept in the dark

12

te siǃa hin ku nǀoaq tcisi ka ku 'm
but they cooked food and ate

ka ha ku 'm tcisi tzanasi
while he ate raw food

14

aia, iin
yes, mother

ǁ'akaa ha tse goaq ǃhai-ǃhai-ǃhai-ǃhai ha te
then he long ago wait, wait, wait, waited for her and he

16

tse ho yaa da'a ko ha dshau khoea
then got fire from his wife

te ha dshau ǀxoa nǃang da'a te
then his wife started the fire and

18

ha tse dcaa hi
he came and stole it

ǁ'a ha te ǁae hi te ǃaah u te hi hin ha ka gǀae tseela
so he took it and ran off and this is the fire he went and took from her

20

gǀae ka gǀae ǀxoa ǁ'akoa
(he) arrived and made fire there

dshau hin kxaice ho da'a
that woman first found fire

22

khama dshau nǀa ǁxoasi a hin ho ka ha o tci nǃa'an
because a woman naturally you see is a big thing

iin
yes

24

mi ǂxae
my daughter

khuin ǀ'ae
that's how it was

26

ka koe te
it was like that and

ǁ'akaa ju ka cuuuu te ka kxae da'a te ku, ku, ku ǀxoa da'a
therefore people have continued to have fire and to, to, to make fire

28

ee, aie
yes, mother
khuin l'ae ka oo khuian
30 *it was like this*
aie
mother
te toan
32 *it's finished*

Chapter 4

The Elephant First Found Water

SUMMARY. The elephant was the one who first found water. He hid it from people and drank it alone. But the mud from the water stuck to his ankles and his wife, the Beautiful Aardvark Girl, asked the others how he could have found water and could be drinking it without sharing. Her husband pretended it was plain sand they were seeing on his ankles. The Aardvark Girl's brothers tracked him and saw him drinking water. When he went off eating trees, they drank up all the water and then filled the waterhole with their piss. When the elephant came back he thought it was plain water and went to drink. But the piss refused. As he turned away, he saw the brothers, who had spent the day making spears, sitting with their sister in their midst. The elephant tried to grab his wife with his trunk, but the brothers stabbed him so that spears met this way and that inside his body and he died. The brothers were little birds, the swallows that come with the rain.

SPEAKER.   *|Asa N!aan*

RECORDED.   Kauri, Botswana, 1971

TRANSCRIBED BY.   *|Ai!ae Fridrick |Kunta, Hacky Kgami Gcao*

ee, haa, aia, ha !xo m kxaice ho ka g!u
yes, he, my mother, the elephant first found water
ee
yes
ha !xo hin tsi kxaina ho ka g!u
the elephant was the one who first found water

2

11

o nǀeʼe te ku tchi ka
he drank it alone

ee
yes

te kaahn ju ko ka te o nǀeʼe te tchi ka te
and hid it from people and drank it alone and

ka g‡kaa hin
that mud

ka g‡kaa ku ǁae ha !ʼhomsi
the mud stuck to his ankles

ka ha u cu
then he went and lay down

ka ha Gǃkunǁʼhomdima ko ʺju hoo,
then Beautiful Aardvark Girl said, ʺpeople,

ju hee, hatce !ʼhoan he kuri ka, ha re o jua ho gǃu he te ku tchi te ǀoa !oa e?ʺ
people, what is it that this man now, is he a person who found water and is drinking without telling us?ʺ

ka ha !ʼhoan !xau
and her husband refused

ka ko ʺmi m ǀoa tchi gǃu
and he said ʺIʼm not drinking water

te kxa ǀʼhoan si hin toʼa te a seʺ
and it is plain sand which you seeʺ

aia, ha koe nǁae
mother, that was what he said

ka
and

g‡ahan te !oa ha !o-sin te ko ʺju hoo,
earlier she had told her brothers and said ʺpeople,

!ʼhoan he o mi ma o ha khoeca ho gǃu he kaahn,
my husband perhaps found water and kept it secret from us,

ku kxuan m.
is being stingy to us.

nǀang i kxoe, m gǁa ha !uh, nǀang
come now, let us follow his spoor, and

gǀae kxoa tca ha ku tchia koa keʺ
go to look for what he is drinking hereʺ

aʼu tsaʼa mi?
do you understand me ?

te aie
and mother

si tuih te g‖a ha !uh te ⎮oo ha te g⎮ae se te ha ǂaeh tchi ka

24 *they stood up and followed his spoor and tracked him and went and saw him and he arrived and was drinking it*

te to'a te !'hu u

and went off gathering

khama jua ku 'm !aihnsi n⎮a

26 *because he is a person who obviously eats trees*

ee aia

yes, mother

ha g⎮ae cu te ku 'm ka !aihnsi te si tsi ǂaeh ‖kae te tchi !hun ka

28 *he spent a long time eating trees and they came together and drank it all up*

te si g⎮xam waqnsi

and all their urine

si g⎮xam g!a'in ‖'a g!u n!ang

30 *they urinated the waterhole full*

te ha 'm, 'm ka g!anisi te haa ⎮am ku ca'an koa ke

and he ate, ate the roots and the sun was going down

ha koh ha ni te, ha ku tsi te se cu ka te khoeca ko g!u ⎮'hoan

32 *he tried, he came and saw it lying there and thought maybe it was plain water*

te tsi ǂaeh te

and came and

ǂ'aia ka ko ‖'a ha xuxua kahinto'a, ha ǂ'ai te

34 *dipped it up with that trunk of his, he dipped it up and*

ko ha tchi te ka koh (clap!) ka !xau

wanted to drink it but (clap!) it refused

te ha n‖haa koh ha n!abi hin te se n⎮ang si tzi

36 *and just as he was turning around he saw the group of them sitting there*

a tsa'a, aie?

you understand, mother?

ha se si tzi, se n⎮ang si te si ca'an koa ke te

38 *he saw their group, saw them sitting and there were many of them*

g‖aan te ku ku'ua !u!usi

(they) had spent the day heating and hammering spearpoints

mi ǂxae

40 *my daughter*

g⎮ae ku se n⎮anga haa dshau ko ha !osin !ka te

went and saw his wife sitting in the midst of her brothers

g!xa ha buxu te koh ha ni ku gu ha dshau

42 *took out his trunk and tried to grab his wife*

ha !osin nǂhaoh te ‖kaea ‖'akoa

her brothers walked and gathered together there

mi ǂxae

44 *my daughter*

mi ǂxae hee
my daughter here

mi ǂxae hee
46 *my daughter here*

ha !osin nǂhaoh te ǁkaea ǁ'akoa te si ko "ee,
her brothers walked and gathered there and they said "yes,

a nǀa o dshau
48 *you are of course a woman*

te nǁaqe gǂhanha ku koh a
and men long ago did bad things to you

te ǁa'ike e!a !hun ha !xo hin ke"
50 *so today we are going to kill this elephant"*

ha !osin
her brothers

koe nǁae te
52 *thus said and*

!u!usi m ǂhoǂhoa khoe, !u!usi m ǂhoǂhoa khoe, !u!usi ka a ku se ka
spears met this way and that inside his body, if you were there watching

ǁ'a tzama mhi sa hi hin he o gǃa hiasi
54 *then these little birds of the rain*

ee
yes

ǁ'a hi sa ku ihin, ka ku ihin
56 *those that swerve this way and that way*

okaa ka hin tsi si koh ku !'ang ha !xo
that's how they stabbed the elephant

te ka, ǁ'a ka hin ke te hi, ǀaake nǃanga ke hi ǀoa ihin
58 *and that's how those birds today swerve this way and that*

mi ǂxae
my daughter

te si gani ǁ'a !xo nǃa'an ha hin tsi to'a
60 *and they rolled over that big elephant there*

ee, aie
yes, mother

te goaq ha ka,
62 *and long ago he,*

ha ka !ai te
he died and

si ko "ee, e!a m !hun a"
64 *they said "yes, we have killed you"*

ka ju ka
and so people have

||'a kahin ke te ju |aa ka ku gu passa ka g|ae ku !hun ha !xo
so today people get a permit and go and kill an elephant

ee, aie
yes, mother

khuin |'ae ha !xo o n‡haoha te ha hin tsi kxaice ho g!u
that"s how the elephant walked and he was the one who first found water

ee, aia
yes, mother

te g!a ka ku cua ha hin tsi n||ae te g!a ka ku cua,
and rain has fallen, this one caused the rain to fall

ka g!a
the rain

ha hin tsi ka ko g!a ka ku cua n|ang ju ku tchi g!u
this one said that rain should fall so people could drink water

ee, aia
yes, mother

te o ha !xo hin tsi
and it was the elephant here

mi ‡xae
my daughter

Chapter 5

The Ostrich and the Tortoise

SUMMARY.   Tortoise and Ostrich were arguing. Tortoise told Ostrich, "If I cook myself, you'll eat me." Ostrich said he would never do that. But Tortoise fooled him into eating from a pot of cooked tortoise eggs. When he learned what he had done, Ostrich vomited, kicked the pot, and has had red, split shins ever since.

SPEAKER.   *N!ani |'Kun*

RECORDED.   Tsumkwe, Namibia, 2006

TRANSCRIBED BY.   *|Ai!ae Fridrick |Kunta, |Ui Charlie N!aici, G‡kao Martin |Kaece*

‡'ang ‖'a ha ‡'angan
the thought that he was thinking
g‡haan ha ‖o'a sa ha dsuu
2
long ago the tortoise and the ostrich
ha ‖o'a sa dsuu n‡uian khoe
the tortoise and the ostrich were arguing
te ha ‖o'a !oa dsuu te ko: "a-o,
4
and the tortoise told the ostrich and said, "you,
otca ka mi g|ae ‖ohm mi |'ae he n|oan mi |'ae okaa a g|ae 'm mi "
if i go chop myself up and cook myself you'll go and eat me "
te ha ko "maooooooooooooooooooo
6
and he said "(exclamation meaning yow)
mia puh koh
ostrich speech meaning I will never do it
mi cin puh koh"
8
I will never do it"

17

ha ko, "N!au, mi g|ae du mi l'ae ka a g|ae 'm mi"
he said, "Man, I'm gonna go fix myself and you're gonna come and eat me "

ha ko "ha se" te kahin ha g|ae ||ohm !hara ha !on!'usi

₁₀ *he said "you'll see" and therefore he went and split his shins*

ce du ||u kxo ka ha, ha ||o'a ‡'aun 'm
go put the pot on the fire again so he, the tortoise must eat

!xau, "|u 'm a"

₁₂ *(he) rejected (that, saying) "(I'll) never eat you"*

te ha kua tsau te
and he immediately got up and

!a'ami te kua sin g|ae n!un te ||u ||'a kxo-a

₁₄ *immediately ran in a circle and just went to stand and put that pot on the fire*

kua ka ha n!usi ha kua du
quickly cooked his eggs

ka sa to'a g|an-g|an kahin ke, ||'aka sa

₁₆ *those red red ones that are here, those*

ha g|ae te ka toan
he came and they were ready

||ua ka te g|ae ku ko ka ha

₁₈ *set the pot on the fire and went and did and then he*

ha ka, ka ku n!om te ha
he then, it was cooking and he

ku haq'are g!u te tsi g|ae se

₂₀ *went to fetch water and came back and saw*

||u ka
the pot sitting on the fire

te n!un

₂₂ *and stood*

khuin ka ha ooa
like this while he was doing

te g|ae n|angan

₂₄ *and went*

||'ai din n!a'aaaaaaaaaan
a bi-i-ig clump of grass (??)

khama ha (?) ha ka !xui te ka ko !uih n‡hao

₂₆ *because he (?)...and it fell scattering*

ha ge ku se
he stood and looked

ko, "jua ||u kxoa ke kah?"

₂₈ *said, "who put this pot on?"*

n!aesi g||a
all was still

"ha ne ǁu kxoa ke?"
"who put this pot on?"

n!aesi gǁa. "ha nǁa jua ǁu k xoa ke"
all was still. "tell me the person who put this pot on"

n!aesi gǁa. " ye,
all was still. "hey,

gǁxun !aro nǀang tci jaan ke he
(let me) put down my yoke and this good thing here

mi 'm tshan
I'll taste

ka tshan kahin ka ke mi ku ko mi ku tshan ka tci"
and taste this stuff here, I say I will taste the thing"

ha te ku tshan
he tasted it

te gu te
and took it and

ko kho nǂau !ha
was eating the meat from the bone

ǀoa o ooa te o ka nǀa'ngsi te ha ko: "ho,
didn't (?) and he said "ho,

mi hin ku ǂhoe a ka n!anga a ko tzi ka 'm a
I here will take you from the fire and set you aside and eat you

ǂhoe na, mi te 'm
take it off the fire for me, I'm going to eat

toan ka te tchi toan ka te !ae ka te tchi"
it all up and drink (the fat) all up and carry it on my shoulders and drink (the fat)"

ha ko "tsxantsxan" ko ǁ'a ǁ'aia te ko: "a re koh ko hatce?
he said "tsxantsxan" (not clear) and said "what did you say?

ha nǁa, ha, ha koh ko a te ǀu 'm mi
tell me, you, you had said that you would not eat me

kaa ne re a ka ku 'm mi re o hatce?"
what is it that now you're eating me?"

te ha ko "waq, waq, waq," ko "hatcece khoe?" te
and he said "waq, waq, waq, said "what is this?" and

tshu tse(tzi?) koara te ha gǀae !aah
vomited (?) and he ran off

kua !oa ha ko ha hin ke gǀae du ke
soon told him saying he would go and

ǁohm !hara ha !on!'usi te du te
chop-split his shins and

ǁu ǁ'a kxoa te ǁ'ahaa koe ǁama te tsi gǀae ko: "yao,
put that pot on and then he came and arrived and said "yow,

ka jia ke kaqe o hatce?" !aih tcaq
what shit is this here?" kicked-spilled

52

g|ae tcaqa ka ku tcaq ka
went and spilled it, spilled it

"yao, aa ni 'm mi, a kah koh..."
"yow, are you going to eat me, you long ago..."

"tcaua, tca mi ku ||aea a.
(emphatically) "no, I'm holding it for you.

54

mia |u 'm a."
I won't eat you."

56

Chapter 6

Springhare Dances

SUMMARY. Springhare was playing and dancing and making a sound like *tcoqm-tcoqm-tcoqm*. The god was watching him and said he would go home and get a dancing skin from his son !Xuma. He came back and tied the dancing skin on Springhare, who danced all day, imitating the sound of the rain. The god said "give me the dancing skin so I can go home–rain is coming." But springhare kept on dancing and dancing and refused to give him the dancing skin. Finally a heavy rain settled in and beat down, and it beat the dancing skin into pieces. The springhare was then afraid and went into a hole. The god took a long hook and pulled the springhare out, and then beat him with a digging stick on the small of his back as people do with springhares today, to kill them.

SPEAKER. *Dahm Ti N!a'an*

RECORDED. Kauri, Botswana, 1971

TRANSCRIBED BY. *Hacky Kgami Gcao, G‡kao Martin |Kaece*

2

ha n|oqm
the springhare
ha n|oqm
the springhare
ku tcxai tci n|ui te ku ko "tcoqm- tcoqm- tcoqm- tcoqm- tcoqm- tcoqm," ha koe n‖ae
was playing around at something and was making a sound like "(onomatop.)," that's what it sounded like

tca tsi ke ha nǀoqm ka ge ka ku 'm ka ko "tcoqm-tcoqm-tcoqm-tcoqm-tcoqm-
tcoqm"
that is what the springhare was doing, eating and making a sound like "(onomatop.)"

ha nǀoqm ge te ku djxani te ku nǁa'ibi ha !xui te ko djxani
the springhare began to dance and was flipping up his tail as he was dancing

te ha tsi-gǀae gǃu'un ha nǀoqm gǃu'un ha nǀoqm gǃu'un ha nǀoqm gǃu'un ha
nǀoqm gǃu'un ha nǀoqm te gǃu'un ha nǀoqm te
*and he came and watched the springhare and watched the springhare and watched the
springhare and watched the springhare and watched the springhare and watched the
springhare and*

ko "a'an,
said "uh-uh,

kxoe, nǀang mi u nǀang
wait, let me go and

gǃa gua mi !'han !Xuma ko
go home and get from my son !Xuma the

ko ǀ'hun-ma
the dancing skin

nǀang tsi-gǀae ǀ'an a nǀang a !uu nǀang djxani nǀang mi gǃu'un a"
*and come back and give it to you so you can tie it on yourself and dance and I can watch
you"*

!aah u te ≠aeh gu ha te
(he) ran off and got it and

nǃo te ce tsi-gǀae te ha cete djxani ǁ'a tca
hurried and came back and he danced it again

tsi-gǀae ǀ'an ha ko ha te ha !uu ha
came back and gave it to him and he tied it on himself

'hm
hmm

ha gǁaan te gǃu'un ha
he spent the day watching him

te ku gǃu'un ha
and watched

ku gǃu'un ha
and watched

ku gǃu'un ha te ka gǃa, ka gǃa taqm
and watched him and the rain, the rain began to fall

Hoq
(onomatop. imitating the sound of the rain)

"yaih, ha m na ǀ'hun-ma, nǀang mi, gǃa, ǀ'an mi, gǃa m ku tsi gǀae" te a !xau
*"hey, give me the dancing skin so I can go home, give it to me, rain is coming" but he
refused*

ku djxani te ku djxani te gǃa khaua te nǀang
he danced and danced and a heavy rain settled in

n‡a'm !'hun, ha n‡a'm ‡homa ha ko ‖oh, ha sin n‖ang te g!u'un n‖oqm te
beat him hard, beat his dancing skin to pieces, he just sat and watched the springhare and

n‖oqm koaq te g‖ae g!a'ama dom
the springhare was afraid and went and entered a hole

g!a n‡a'm !hun ha te ha !oe g!xa te g!a
the rain beat him hard and he left there and went home

n!o te gu
hurried and grabbed

‖'a, Mama, ‖'a g‡uia he ju ka ku n!ham ha ka du oo ha gu ‖'a g‡uia
now granddaughter, the springhare hook people use today to pull out springhares , he took that springhare hook

gu ‖'a !aia
took that digging stick

tsi-g‖ae te ha cete du ‖'a tca te ha
came and he again did that and he

khu te g‖ae n‡au koa ke te ha g!xuni ha te ko "‖ahn"
jumped and went over here and he beat him with the digging stick and it went "(onomatop.)"

ko ha zuhn te !'ang !'oan ha te !ao ha
on the small of his back and knocked him down

m
mm

ee
yes

ee
yes

mama ee
granddaughter, yes

ee
yes

ee
yes

Chapter 7

Ducks and People

SUMMARY.   The ducks were at first people, and were washing themselves in the water. A man saw them and said to his people, "Let's go look at these things in the waterhole: maybe they're people." The others said, "No, those are animals, not people." But the man wanted to go near them, to go and eat them. So he and his people went into the midst of the ducks. The ducks bit them and pecked them and they all cried out and ran scattering. The ducks then again became people, and went on living.

SPEAKER.   *N!ani |'Kun*

RECORDED.   Tsumkwe, 2006

TRANSCRIBED BY. *|Ui Charlie N!aici, |Ai!ae Fridrick |Kunta*

yaa, yaa n|habite n|a
the, the ducks, now
hi hin he te tsi te hi sa o n|habite n|a hi !xare ge te hi !xare ce ge
2   *they were the ones who came, and of those who are ducks, there are some kinds and then there are other kinds*
te cete o Ju|'hoansi
and they were also Ju|'hoansi (people)
'mhm
4   *mm-hmm*
te ku ‖ka ka g!u
and were washing themselves in the water
ku ‖ka ka g!u te
6   *and were washing themselves in the water and*

25

ǁ'a haa nǀe'esi, xare ha hin
so he alone, even this one

ku nǃun ka ku khuin ha ku ooa siǃa
was standing and this is what he was doing to them

ha, ha, ha se
he, he, he saw

nǀhabite ku djxa ka gǃu
ducks swimming in the water

cete ku ǃoa siǃa
again told them

"a-hoo, tcisa ke gea gǃu nǃang mǃa se"
"you there, let's look at these things that are in the waterhole"

te ko "a-hoo, ju ǁam khoeca hi to'a"
and said "you, maybe in fact those are people over there"

"a-an, ǀoa o ju, ǃha hin to'a"
"uh-uh, they're not people, those are animals"

haa yaa
yes

"m taa ǂaeh gǃa'ama
"we're going to go among them

haa yaa
yes

gǀae 'm"
go and eat them"

te tsi ǂaeh te ka si ku gǃa'ama tsi, gǃa'ama hi
and they went there and when they arrived they went into the midst of them

te yaa, yaa nǀhabite ku se si
and the, the ducks looked at them

okaa hi khoara
it was that most of them came(?)

te gǃhooa si
and were sitting on them

he ku nǃai si te
and biting them and

ku ǁohm he ku nǃai te
then pecking them and biting them and

ku ǁohm te ku nǃai te si sin gǃhoo, te ju gǃxa sarakhoe te ǃaah u
pecking them and biting them and just sitting on them, and the people jumped apart scattering and ran off

si ce te gǀae o Juǀ'hoansi
they again became people

te gǀae ku ǁxam
and went on living

ee
yes
tcisi wece n|a n!ausi ku koe n≠oahn
all these things the old people told us like this
te du
and did
'mhm
mm-hmm

Chapter 8

The Sun's Child

SUMMARY.   When the sun was a person, she roasted a tortoise and shared it with her son. But the son wanted to eat it all himself and began to cry. The sun left him in the shade while she went off gathering raisin berries. When she returned he was still crying but would not let her pick him up. So the sun said, "Because of your refusal I am going to leave you." She tucked her skin cloak between her legs and jumped up into the sky and became the sun. Her child became the white-bellied sunbird who continually cries "Wah, wah, wah!"

SPEAKER.   *Di‖xao Pari |Kai*

RECORDED.   Kauri, Botswana, 1971

TRANSCRIBED BY.   *Hacky Kgami Gcao, |Ui Charlie N!aici, G‡kao Martin |Kaece*

te ka ha |am o Ju|'hoan
and when the sun was a Ju|'hoan (a human being)
ha tsi g|ae ho zam
she came and saw a tortoise
zam he o !ha
this tortoise that is meat
te ‖'akaa ha
and then she
ha |am tsehe
the sun then
g|ae sau ha zam
went and roasted the tortoise
khama |am n|a o |am
because the sun is the sun

29

te tsi g|ae

8

and she went

ha, sa, ha ‖ae

she, they two, she took

da'ama te sa g|ae sau ha zam

10

her child and the two of them went to roast the tortoise

te g!hoo te ku 'm

and sat and were eating (it)

te ha da'ama tse ku tjin

12

and her child then began to cry

ku tjin, te ku tjin, te ku tjin te ha taqe kua

cried, and cried, and cried and his mother immediately

te ha taqe ku ko: "da'amaa ne xae he

14

and his mother said, "what (kind of) child is this

te koe tjin kxui wa?"

who is crying this way?"

kua n‖aahan ha ko khuin to'a o !hari

16

immediately left him in the shade

ka ha ku n‖aahan ha ko !hari

when she left him in the shade

ha g|ae n!un te ku

18

she went and stood and

ku 'm ka tcisi

was eating things

'm n|ang

20

she ate raisin berries

te da'ama gea khuin to'a o !hari te ka !om g‖xun ha |'ae

and the child was there in the shade and had buried himself

ko, ko kxa

22

with, with sand

te ku tjin, te ku tjin, te ku tjin te ha taqe cete u ce

and cried, and cried, and cried and his mother came back again

te ko ha gu ha te ha !xau

24

and wanted to pick him up but he refused

te ha cete n‖aahn ha te u

so she left him again and went away

te ka ha ku n‖aahn ha ku u

26

and when she left him and went away

‖'akaa ha cete u n!un te 'm te

then she again went and stood and was eating and

'm te ku 'm te ha da'ama

28

was eating and eating and her child

cua khuin to'a te tjin
was lying there and crying

te ha da'ama tjin, tjin, tjin te ka ha ka u ‖ama ‖'akoa ku tsi ǂaeha !hari

30　*and her child cried, cried, cried and when she was coming from there and arrived at the shade*

tsi ǂaeh ko ha gu ha da'ama te da'ama ku !xau te ha...
arrived and wanted to pick up her child but the child refused and she...

"ehee, ka a koe !xau okaa mi ka n‖aahn a"

32　*"yes, since you are refusing I am going to leave you"*

te ka g‖ae kua gu, ha n|a koh kxae
and went and immediately took, she of course had

tci-tcia khuin |'ae ka khuian

34　*something (garment) like this*

te kua g‖ae nǂaba ka
and immediately went and folded it between her legs

‖'aha te khu, g!a'ama u n|a'an

36　*then she jumped, went right up into the sky*

te da'ama tia !aua khuin to'a
and the child itself remained there

to'a te u te ‖'aha ha te ka g‖ae o

38　*she went off and left and has become*

|am
the sun

‖u te ha hin he te o |am

40　*hangs in the sky and she is the sun*

te ha da'ama ka !aia khuin to'a
and her child died there

sa–ha !aia khuin to'a

42　*they two–he died there*

ha taqe ka g‖ae o |am
his mother has become the sun

aia

44　*mother*

te |am da'ama o tzamama
and the sun's child is a little bird

ee

46　*yes*

tzamama to'a he ha tzi gǂa'in he koe
that little bird that has a long beak like this

ee

48　*yes*

he djo
and (it is) black

50 oasi te ko "waqaan,
    his custom is to say "(onomatop.),

    hiaqaan, waqaan, waqaan,
    (onomatop.)

52 waqaan," ka ‖u ka ku tjin
    (onomatop.)," and perches and cries

    o a he, o ǀamma
    it is this one, the sunbird (white-bellied sunbird, Cinnyris talatala)

    o ha ǀama he, ‖'a da'ama
54 *it is the sun's child*

    o ǀama
    it is the sun's

    ‖'a ha da'ama
56 *child*

Chapter 9

The Tamsa Bird

SUMMARY.   The god had married two women who were birds, the grey hornbill
and the yellow-billed hornbill. He dug *g‖xaru* (Lapeirousia bainesii)
roots, and filled a sack with them. The god was a person who did
not share food with his wives, so he hung up the sack, pretending
it was filled with sand. They all danced, and he secretly ate *g‖xaru*
from the sack. He also prepared a long wooden paddle and laid it by.
When they danced again, the god said he didn't want his wives to
dance in front of him, but instead he wanted the tall woman sitting
on the other side of the fire. The tall woman paid him no mind, but
just kept on singing. Another woman came to dance in front of him,
but he refused, calling again for the tall woman. Again she refused.
Much later the tall woman, her bangles clinking, came and danced
with him. They danced in parallel, and then sat down and turned
away from and towards each other in turn. Then the god took up
his long wooden paddle and beat her stomach and threw her down
and she died. The dance split up and the god was alone, praising
himself and saying, "This is how I do things!"

SPEAKER.   *‖Xoan N!a'an*

RECORDED.   Kauri, Botswana, 1971

TRANSCRIBED BY.   *Tsamkxao Fanni ‖Ui, Jafet Gcao Nqeni, G‡kao Martin ‖Kaece*

ha koh n‖hui dshau tsaqn sa
he had married two women who
ju ku ko ha n‖ui
people say that one of them

2

33

te,
(was,)

ha n|ui hin to'a he o ǂhamsa
one of them was the grey hornbill, Tockus nasutus

te ha hin to'a o ha, ee
and this one was the, yes

ha g!u ka gǂa'in, ha ku ko "tcaqri, tcaqri, tcaqri, tcaq'in, tcaq
her stomach was long, she said "(onomatop.)

tcaq'in, tcaq'in, tcaq'in, tcaq'intcaq'in"
(onomatop)

he khoe tcu he ha hin to'a
and was like the yellow-billed hornbill (Tockus flavirostris) here, that one

ee, tsi ho ha dshaua he o Ju|'hoandi he ju ku ko "hatce ce khoe to'a?"
yes, came and saw this woman here, a Ju|'hoan woman that people said "what was that there?"

"hatce ce ǁu ce hatce?"
"what again perched here is what?"

ǁu care...
perched facing...

te ǁxoasi
and naturally

te
and

ha gu gǁxaru, te gu gǁxaru, te gu gǁxaru te
he dug gǁxaru (roots of Lapeirousia bainesii), and dug gǁxaru, and dug gǁxaru and

sa ka n|aisi can khoe sa hinke ha gu
whose bulbs were this big, he dug

te gu te
and dug and

tsau
got up

ǁ'aha te |'u g!a'in !oma
and he filled up the sack

khama jua |oa 'm |xoa ha dshausin he |oa 'm |xoa ju
because he was a person who did not eat with his wives, he didn't eat with people

ha ku g|ae ǁu ka
he went and hung it up

"mtsa nǂhao ǁkae
"let us two walk together

te tse ku djxani ka tcxai"
and then dance a dance"

mm
yes

24 te dshau he
and this woman

dshaua to'a, kohm, ǀoe tsi gǀae
that woman, for sure, just came up

26 gǁxaru tse taa koe
the gǁxaru itself came to lie like this

ha nǀhui ka n!ani te ǁ'a te
he took three of them and then

28 tsau te !'un kxa
stood up and picked up handfuls of sand

kxa sa ka hin ke ha !'un te
this sand here he picked up by handfuls and

30 ǀ'u ha !oma, ǀ'u ha !oma, ǀ'u ha !oma
put it into the bag, put it into the bag, put it into the bag

nǁa te ko ha gǁxaru te ha nǀhui ka gǁxaru n!ani
mentioned the gǁxaru and took three gǁxaru

32 te ǀ'ua khoe nǀui
and put them somewhere else

te ǂaeh ku djxani, ǂaeh te si ge'e
and went home and danced, went home and they sang

34 ha djxani te djxani te tsi !'an ko ha ni gu ka gǁxaru nǀang 'm te
he danced and danced and went forward and tried to take the gǁxaru and eat and

te coe ka n!ani te 'm
and took out three and ate them

36 te ko ha te nǀhui ka kxa
and said he had pulled out sand

te kua gu ǁ'a !aihnǀ'o he kahin to'a he o ha ga
and quickly took that wooden paddle there of his

38 te
and

ǂaeh cu te
went back and lay down and

40 " zain, zain, zain
(sings) onomatop

zain, zain, zain
(onomatop)

42 zain, zain, zain, zain, zain, zain"
(onomatop.)"

ka ha
and then he

44 ha dshau nǀui
another woman

‡hom ka
ended it (the song)

ka ha dshau nǀui ‡hom ka ǁ'aka ha ka nǀang ka ku
and then another woman ended it and she sat and was

tsi ‡aeha ha ka ha ko "ǀ'aeqe"
going to come to him but he said "(onomatop)"

"mi ǁa'ike ǀoa kxoa ju sa he
"today I don't want these people

te ku kxoa dshaua gǀae to'a nǀang
but I want that woman sitting on the other side over there

te g‡a'in
who is tall

mi m ku kxoa ǁ'a dshaua"
I want that woman"

ka ǁ'a dshaua ǀoe nǃun ka ku ge'e
and that woman just stood and was singing

ka
and

ka
and

ka
and

ka si !hun ǁ'a tzia
and they killed (ended) that song

ka ce ka gu tsau
and then began again

ka ha ‡aeh n‡hao ka cu ka du
and then he went and dropped down and lay down and was doing

ǁ'a tca
that

ka dshau nǀui gǀai ka tsi ‡aeha
and another woman came out and came up to him

ka tsi ‡aeh ku nǀamm
and came up and danced before him

te ha ko "ǀ'hain
and he said "(onomatop.lisping speech)

"ǀ'hain te ǀxau sa dshau...
"(onomatop. and refuse that woman (lisping speech)...

dshau sa he ǁa'ike ku ‡aeha mi he
these women who today are coming to me....

dshau u he, mi tia kxoa dshaua u he ka ka ha nǀamm mi"
that woman over there, I myself want that woman over there to dance in front of me"

66 ha koe n‖ae
he thus spoke

ha
he

68 te si ‖oe ‖oa ko te ku ko te ha ku koe n‖ae te
but they just didn't say (anything)and they just did and he thus said

!hun ‖'a tzia
(they) killed that song

70 te
and

te ‖oe ku koe djxani
and just danced like this

72 te ku
and was

dshausi ku n‖amm ha
women were dancing in front of him

74 ha ku !xau
he refused

te ‖'a dshaua
and that woman

76 !aihn te tsi ǂaeha
was clinking (bangles) and came up to him

te sa ǂaroa khoe te khuin l'ae sa u g!hooa te ha
and they two danced parallel to each other and thus they went and sat and he

78 ha ku mania ha l'ae ko ha dshau, ka ku mani ha l'ae, ka dshau ku mani hal'ae
he turned himself toward the woman, and turned back, and then the woman turned her

l'ae ko ha ka ha ku mania ha l'ae ko ha dshau
self towards him and then he turned himself toward the woman

80 te ha n‖a ‖ae ‖'a !aihnl'oa, ha kua ko " ǂhoan" ko ha tchin‖ho
and he certainly held that wooden paddle, and quickly went "(onomatop.)" on her midriff

te n!o'an nǂhao
threw her down

82 te !ai
and (she) died

aie, te ka tcxai ka, ju ka, ka tcxai ka saraa khoe ko khuin to'a
mother, and the dance then, people then, the dance then split up there

84 mm
yes

te ju kxae, ju ka
and people had, people had

86 g‖ae te ha kare ha l'ae te ko
gone and he praised himself and said

"|'haqn |'haqn tia koe"
"(onomatop) myself thus"
tca tcisa ||'a ||'aiha n!a'an n||aahn du
88
that which, things that that old god long ago did
o tcisa ju !ae n||aahn ku n||ae he mi ku tsa'a
they're the things the old people long ago told that I heard
mm
90
yes

Chapter 10

Tug-of-War

SUMMARY. ǀ'Oma ǀ'Oma, a Juǀ'hoan man, had the first cattle and herded them alone, but they had no kraal. A Black man came and asked whose cattle they were. The Juǀ'hoan man said they were his, but agreed to herd them back to the village with the Black man to spend the night. One of the cows had given birth, so the Black man said, "Let's milk her and taste the milk." ǀ'Oma ǀ'Oma was afraid of the cow, so he asked the Black man to tie her up with a leather riem. The Black man told ǀ'Oma ǀ'Oma to wash the pot so they could cook the milk and eat it together. But ǀ'Oma ǀ'Oma refused, saying the other should drink the milk and he would scrape the pot. Then ǀ'Oma ǀ'Oma gave the Black man a leather riem that was tied to a piece of string. The two of them pulled on its opposite ends. It soon broke, and the Black man got the riem, while ǀ'Oma ǀ'Oma got the string. The Black man said he would keep the cows and the Juǀ'hoan man would be his servant. ǀ'Oma ǀ'Oma had to go off and eat little things like the three kinds of raisin berries, and the Black man began to cultivate sorghum and maize and ate them along with beef and milk.

SPEAKER. *Diǁxao Pari ǀKai*

RECORDED. Kauri, Botswana, 1971

TRANSCRIBED BY. *Tsamkxao Fanni ǀUi, Hacky Kgami Gcao, ǀAiǃae Fridrick ǀKunta*

khama ha nǀa o jua koh koe du te
because he was certainly a person who did thus and
ka ha ku koe du ǁ'akaa ha tse
² *and he did thus and then he*

39

sa goba
and the black person

ha nǀa ko gumi sa koh kxaina o ha hisi
he (ǀʼOma ǀʼOma) certainly said cattle first belonged to him

khama ha hin koh o ǁʼaixa
because he was a rich person

koa ha ǁama
from his origin

ha koh o ǁʼaiha
he was a rich person

khama ha te, ha hin tsi o haa, ha nǀa u ha hin he
because he, he was that, he went that side

te ka ha o ǁʼaiha ǁʼakaa ha tsi gǀae
and when he was a rich man he came

te gumi hi nǀa koh koara !hua
but the cattle certainly had no kraal

ha tsi gǀae
he came

ha tsi gǀae te sa tsi gǀae du hi te du hi te du hi te ha o nǀeʼe te du hi te
he came and they came and herded the cattle, and herded them, and herded them and he alone herded them

iin, te tsi gǀae nǀang !hari
yes, and went to sit in the shade

te ha goba nǀui ǁama te tsi gǀae, goba
and a black man came there, a black man

"tcisa ke re o tcisa o hajoe gasi?"
"whose things (animals) are these?"

te ha koh "tcisa o mi gasi"
and he said "these are my things"

"ihin, te ka ka o a gasi, re
"yes, and if they are yours, why

mtsa du hi nǀang ǁʼa mtsa te du ua hi ko tjuǀho?"
not herd them so that we can drive them back to the village?"

sa, sa kua zaihan khoe
they, they soon agreed

kua du hi te du hi te tani ua hi ko tjuǀho
soon herded them and herded them and brought them back to the village

te ka sa ku tani ua hi ko tjuǀho
and when they brought them to the village

sa nǀuia toʼa ǁʼa ha kua !oa ha te ko–kana ha nǀui te ǁamm–
his colleague there soon told him and said–because one of them had given birth–

kua !oa ha te ko, "haa mtsa ǂaeh tzao tca ke
soon told him and said, "you, let's go milk this thing

nǀang tsi gǀae tsaahn"
and then go taste it"

ha ko "ee, to'a, nǀang mtsa u ǂaeh tzao"
he said "yes, go, let's go arrive and milk"

te ha ko, sa ku gǀae te ha ko
and he said, they went and he said

"mi m ku mi, ha, haa ǁ'ang ha, mi m ku koaq ha"
"I'm going to, I, you, you tie it up, I'm afraid of it"

(ǀUi ma, a m gǂom, itsa gǂom gǃhoo, gǂom i tzisi nǀang gǃhoo)
(ǀUi ma, you be quiet, you two be quiet, silence your mouths and sit down)

"mi ku koaq ha, nǀa a ǁ'ang ha"
"I'm afraid of it, now you tie it up"

haa ǀ'Oma ǀ'Oma ha nǀa koh koaq ha
ǀ'Oma ǀ'Oma certainly was afraid of it

he ku ko ha u he ha ǁ'ang ha
and he said the other one should go and tie him up

ha tsi gǀae gu xore te tsi gǀae ǁ'ang ha
he came and got a riem and came and tied it up

te nǀang te tzao
and sat down and milked

tzao ha tzao ha te tia ka tzao gǃa'in tan
milked it and milked it and milked the dish full

ka gǃa'in te ha ǁama
it was full and he came from there

sa tsi ǃ'an te ha ko, ha ǀ'Oma ǀ'Oma ne ǃoa ha te ko
they two came up and he said, ǀ'Oma ǀ'Oma told him, saying

"ǁka kxoa to'a nǃun,
"wash the pot that is standing there,

nǀang nǀoaq
and cook

nǀang mtsa, mtsa tsaahn "
so we two, we two can taste it"

te ha ko
and he said

ha goba nǃau nǃa'an ko "a re
the old black man said "are you

a re, tca ke re a re ǃ'han wa?"
do you, do you know this thing?"

"'In-in, mi m ǀoa ǃ'han tca ke,
"no, I don't know this thing,

mia o ǀ'Oma ǀ'Oma m ǀoa ǃ'han ka"
I, ǀ'Oma ǀ'Oma, certainly do not know it"

"ha n|a a kho"
"now you wait"

46

te ha ka
and he

haa |'Oma |'Oma ‖ka ka ‖ka ka kxo te ‖ka ka te sa kua n|oaq
|'Oma |'Oma washed and washed the pot and washed it and they soon cooked

48

te ka kua tsi g|ae koe buxobe
and it soon became like porridge

sa kua ǂhoe ka te n!ang ka te ka ǂa'u
they two quickly took it off the fire and set it down and it cooled

50

te sa
and they two

sa n|ui ko "te a re ca hoe ka mtsa 'm?"
the other one said, "will you come so the two of us can eat?"

52

te ha ko 'in-in", ha |'Oma |'Oma kua !xau, ko "'in-in,
and he said " uh-uh," |'Oma |'Oma quickly refused, and said "uh-uh,

'm tca to'a n|ang 'm ‖'a a te nǂai n‖o'ma mi"
"eat that, eat that and let me scrape the pot"

54

sa 'm te ha to'a kua 'm te 'm te 'm te 'm te kua gu kxo n!ang te
they ate and that one quickly ate and ate and ate and ate and soon took the rest of the pot

kxo te |'an ha
and gave the pot to him

56

ha kua, ha n|a n|ang te n‖o'm ka
he quickly, he certainly sat down and scraped it

n‖o'm te n‖o'm te n‖o'm te n‖o'm te sa kua tuih g‖a
scraped and scraped and scraped and scraped and they two soon stood up

58

te ha kua ko
and he quickly said

"gu xore
"take the riem

60

n|ang mi gu !hui"; haa |'Oma |'Oma n|a gu !hui
and let me take the string"; |'Oma |'Oma certainly took the string

te ha goba gu xore
and the black man took the riem

62

te sa kua
and they soon

‖haia khoe ko ‖'a !huia kahinto'a
pulled on opposite ends of that string

64

te !hui kua ǂhom
and the string soon broke

ka !hui ku ǂhom ‖'akaa |'Oma |'Oma tse
the string broke so that |'Oma |'Oma then

g‖ae ku !aah n≠au tzi
went and ran into the bush

te ha goba
and the black man

ha goba tse kua ku !aah tsi ≠aeh khuinke he o ‖'hai
the black man then soon ran and arrived here in the east

ha ka !oa haa, ha goba ka !oa ha te ko, "ee,
he certainly told him, the black man told him and said, "yes,

to'a u
go away

gumi sa he o gumi sa ka o mi hisi
these cows here are cows that will be mine

mi ka kxae, te a ka ku taokhomm
I will keep them and you will be ashamed

te a ka o mi g‖aakhoe"
and you will be my servant"

sa kua n≠haoh saraa khoe
they soon went their separate ways

te ha g‖ae !aah u te haa goba kua !aah tsi ≠aeh
and he ran off and the black man soon ran home

ee, te ha to'a g‖ae 'm tci dore sin
yes, and that one went and ate bad things

o tcisa kahinke he o n‖ang he o kaqa'amakoq he o, o g!oan
these things like raisin berries, two-color raisinberries, and Kalahari raisinberries

sa ‖'Oma ‖'Oma hin ka g‖ae 'm
that this ‖'Oma ‖'Oma went to eat

te ha goba ka tsi ≠aeh ge te ‖xarah
and the black man began to cultivate

ko mabare !ansi te ko camanga sin te
things like sorghum and maize and

ka ko gumi sa hin to'a te
and also these cattle and

te ka ku 'm
began to eat them

te haa ‖'Oma ‖'Oma ‖'a ha ka g‖ae u
and ‖'Oma ‖'Oma went away

te g‖ae o g‖aakhoe
and became a servant

iin
yes

ee
yes

ee, ka za'a n!om tsau
yes, it's already finished

88

Chapter 11

Eyes-on-his-Ankles

SUMMARY.   Two men were digging g‖xaru (Lapeirousia bainesii) roots. One of them was named Eyes-on-his-Ankles. At night they lay down to sleep. The other man saw that Eyes-on-his-Ankles had no eyes on his face, and wondered where his eyes were. He flicked sand on his face but no eyes blinked. He flicked sand on his wrists, but no eyes blinked there. Then he flicked sand on his ankles, and there, the eyes blinked. "Aha," he said, "are this person's eyes placed on his ankles?" They slept and in the morning went to dig g‖xaru again. When the sun was going down, the man told Eyes-on-his-Ankles to drop his g‖xaru and let him roast it. Then he went and chopped a long wooden paddle, and put it into the fire to heat. Meanwhile Eyes-on-his-Ankles was wrapping up his g‖xaru in little bundles and coming back and dropping it for the man to roast, but was trying to stand far away. Nevertheless the man burned his eyes with the hot fire paddle so that they split open, and knocked him down and roasted him along with the g‖xaru.

SPEAKER.   *|Xoan N!a'an*

RECORDED.   Kauri, Botswana, 1971

TRANSCRIBED BY.   *Tsamkxao Fanni |Ui, Hacky Kgami Gcao, |Ai!ae Fridrick |Kunta*

jua du tcisa ǂhai, te ‖am
a person who did lots of things, for sure
ǂ'ang
thought
ha ‖a'i n|ui ce ka
one day he again

2

45

si!aa
they all

4

si!a g|ae, si!a g|ae
they all, they all went

gu ka g‖xaru ka gu ka g‖xaru ka gu ka g‖xaru ka gu ka g‖xaru ka haa !'Hom-!'hom-tzi-g|a'asi
(and) dug Lapeirousia bainesii–food plant root–and dug it and dug it and dug it and then Eyes-on-his-Ankles

6

ehee
yes

te
and

8

haa !'Homtzig|a'asi te
Eyes-on-his-Ankles (short form of name) then

‖'a haa
then he

10

sa ku, sa ku sau ka
they two, they two were roasting it

sa n|a saua ka ko tzi
they two certainly roasted it in the bush

12

ee
yes

ka sa ku sau ka, ka ha
and then they two roasted it, and then he

14

ha ku
he was

okaa ha
it was that he

16

okaa g|u
it was night

sa g≠a
they two lay down

18

ha ku !hai ka
he was waiting for

kxoni ka kxa ka du
preparing the sand and did it

20

ku du se ha, "jua he re ha g|a'asi g‖a kore?
was trying him out, "where are this person's eyes?

ha g|a'asi re o kore?
where are his eyes?

22

ha g|a'asi re g‖a kore?"
where are his eyes placed?"

ka ihin kxa
then did thus with sand

24

ka du khoe nǀui, ka ka ǀoa tatabe
and did it some more, and they didn't blink

ka ha tam
so he didn't know

26

ka ko, "ka ke ha ǁho hin ke..."
and said, "that this is his face here..."

ka ce ka gu ka, ka naq'am ka gua ka
and took it again, took it (how?)

28

du ha ǁho ka, ka ǀoa tatabe
did his face but, but (his eyes) didn't blink

"ha gǀa'asi re gǁa kore?"
"where are his eyes placed?"

30

te ǁ'akaa ha
and then he

ka tsi gǀae du ha ha, ha g‡aisi
and then came to do his, his wrists

32

ka ka ǀoa tatabe
but they didn't blink

"jua he re ha gǀa'asi gǁa kore?"
"where are this person's eyes placed?"

34

te ǁ'a ha te koh kah ce koh
and then he did it and again did it

ha !'hom tzi sa kahinke
(to) his ankles here

36

ha ihin
he thus did

te ihin te ha gǀa'asi taa...
and went like this and his eyes themselves...

38

"jua he ǁoeh ha gǀa'asi re gǁa khuin ke wa?"
"are this person's eyes in fact placed here?"

aie
mother

40

"ehee, ha gǀa'asi re ǁoeh gǁa khuin ke?"
"aha, are his eyes in fact placed here?"

te kua
and quickly

42

kua !oa ha te ko
quickly told him and said

"mtsa m, okaa ha...
"we two, it is when he...

44

mtsa, mtsa ka ku tza"
we two, we two are going to sleep"

46
'mhmm
yes

te sa
and they two

48
"mtsa tza ka n!homa-n|o ka g|ae
"we two are going to sleep and tomorrow will go

g|ae, g|ae gu ka g‖xaru"
go, go dig g‖xaru roots (Lapeirousia bainesii)"

50
‖'a ha koe n‖ae te sa tza te n!o te
then he thus spoke and they two slept and in the morning

g|ae gu ka g‖xaru te gu ka g‖xaru te gu ka g‖xaru te
went to dig g‖xaru and dug g‖xaru and dug g‖xaru and

52
|'u yaa da'a
built a fire

ha m, aie
yes, mother

54
te gu ka g‖xaru te gu ka g‖xaru te
and dug g‖xaru and dug g‖xaru and

ha |am ka ku ca'an koa ke
the sun had come to lie here (low on horizon)

56
te sa tsi ǂaeh
and they two arrived

te !xoana ka g‖xaru te !xoana te !xoana
and lived by the g‖xaru (patch) and lived and lived

58
ha tse !oa ha te ko "!'Hom!'homtzig|a'asi, n|a a ka |'u taqm g‖xaru n|ang mi sau"
he then told him and said "Eyes-on-his-Ankles, now you should drop your g‖xaru and let me roast it"

ha hin ‖'a kaoha ‖'a ha o kxuisi hin ke
these here were the words of this one, the god

60
"|'u taqm ka g‖xaru n|ang mi ka sau ka"
"put down the g‖xaru and let me roast it"

te ha g|ae ‖ohm !aihn-|'oa caan khuinke
and he went and chopped a wooden paddle that was this big

62
inn
yes

te
and

64
ha ku
he was

ha ku !oqm ka g‖xaru ka tsi g|ae ko ha ni n!un ǂxan ku taqm ka ha
he was wrapping up the g‖xaru and came and tried to stand far away while he was dropping (it) and he

ha taqm ka
he dropped it

ka ce ka g|ae !oqm ka tsi g|ae taqm
and then went to wrap it up again and came and dropped it

ka ce g|ae !oqm ka tsi g|ae taqm
and went again to wrap it up and then came and dropped it

te g!a !oqma din n!ang te ku tsi g|ae, te ha...
and went and wrapped up the last of it and was coming, and he...

"hatce re a ‖a'ike ku !oqm
"how is it that you are today wrapping

g‖xaru ka n!un ǂxaan ka ku taqm ne o hatce?
g‖xaru and standing far off and dropping it, is what?

ka a |oa n!un to'ma mi kae ma o hatce?"
that you don't stand close to me is what?"

‖'a ha ku khoe tsitsa'a kxui ha !'Hom!'homtzig|a'asi
then he was thus going about asking Eyes-on-his-Ankles

te
and

ha n|a ǂ'ai ‖'a !aihn|'oa ko
he certainly dipped that wooden paddle into

ko yaa da'a te ‖ae
into the fire and held it

te ‖'akaa ha tse
and then he

ka ha ǂaeh ku ǂ'ai ka ‖'akaa ha tse
and when he went and dipped it, then he

ha tse ku taqm ka g‖xaru te ha tse
he came and dropped the g‖xaru and then he

xaba ka ha g|a'asi ko yaa da'a
shoveled the fire over his eyes

te yaa da'a tse ku'u
and the fire burned

ku'u !'oahn ha te
burnt him down and

!ao ha
knocked him down

te ha g|a'asi ku'u !hara
and his eyes were burned until they split

‖'akaa ha tse kua
and then he quickly

86
du ha te du ha te du ha
did him and did him and did him

sau |xoa ha ko ka g‖xaru
roasted him with the g‖xaru

88
inn
yes

te sau te
and roasted and

90
‖'akaa ha tse goaq du te
then he long ago did and

du ‖'a !ha te ko ka g‖xaru te ko ka !ha, te ‖'akaa ha tse koah ‖ae te tse g|ae u
did that meat and took the g‖xaru together with the meat and then he soon afterward
picked it up and then went off

92
tjin n≠au ka tju‖ho
went off crying to the village

ee
yes

94
!'Hom!'homtzig|a'asi
Eyes-on-his-Ankles

Chapter 12

The Two Boys and the Lions

SUMMARY.   The god had two sons, !Xuma and Kha‖'an. The boys went hunting and killed an eland. Lions came and killed the boys in turn, and buried them in the eland's stomach contents (chyme). The father was helped to track the boys by a turtle who put his head into the coals of the fires they had made along their journey. At the last fire the coals were hot, and the turtle's head was burned, so they knew the eland's death place was nearby. When they reached it, the god immediately saw that his sons were buried in the chyme, but pretended he couldn't see them. He asked pied babbler birds and other birds to sing, but the boys didn't come out of the chyme. Then he asked all the animals in turn to dance, but his children still did not emerge. So he hung a meteor, "this fire that hangs in the sky and kills people", up in a tree. When he called the meteor down onto the eland's death place, it blasted through the chyme and !Xuma and Kha‖'an jumped out. They cooked the eland meat and ate well. They took the rest of the meat home and the lions had none.

SPEAKER.   ǀXoan N!a'an

RECORDED.   Kauri, Botswana, 1971

TRANSCRIBED BY. *Beesa Crystal Boo, Tsamkxao Fanni ǀUi, Hacky Kgami Gcao, ǀAi!ae Fridrick ǀKunta*

ka nǀui cete o
another one is
haa, ha hin ‖'a ha ‖'aiha
²   *he, this one who was god*

51

haa ‖'aiha ‖'a ha mhisi, !Xuma keti... ha ‖'aiha ‖'a ha mhisi
god's sons, !Xuma and... god's sons

!Xuma

4
!Xuma

te o Kha‖'an
and Kha‖'an

ehee

6
yes

te ‖'a da'abi sa to'a tse
and those children then

u !aqe

8
went hunting

ha mhisi
his sons

te tse u !hun n!ang

10
and they went and killed an eland

inn
yes

te tse,tse tza ha khoea

12
and went, went and slept (where it died)

te tse ku du ha
and then were doing it

te du ha te

14
and doing it

haa n!hai
the lion

haa n!hai ‖'a ha tse

16
the lion then

ha tse
he then

ha tse tsi g‖ae, tsi g‖ae !'oan sa

18
he then came, came and killed them

ee, !'oan sa waqn toan si
yes, killed both of them

te haa n!ang g!u zi ha tse !oma sa

20
and he buried the two in the eland's stomach contents

ee
yes

‖'a ha tse gea ‖'akoa te tse ku 'm ka !ha

22
then he came and stayed there and then was eating the meat

ee
yes

te ha ba tse
and his father then

24

si!a ba tse ge te kxoa ha kxoa si kxoa si kxoa si kxoa si kxoa si
their father then looked for him, looked for them, looked for them, looked for them, looked for them

ǀoa ho si
didn't find them

26

ee
yes

te ǁa'i nǀui nǀhui si
and one day took them

28

te !'oahn si te ko zam sin te
and opened them–and there were turtles

ǁo'a sin te
and tortoises and

30

tcisi waqn to'an si sin te
all these things and

ǁae si
took them

32

te si!a tse ku ǀoo si
and they all followed them

sa !uh
their track

34

ǁxam ǁxam ka tsi se koa sa tza
went along and went along and came and saw where they had slept

ka ha !oa zam ka ko
then he told the turtle and said

36

"ǀ'u a nǀai ko
put your head in

koa ke ko
here, in the

38

da'a hee
fire here

da'a he re hi n!ang ǂa'u?"
is the inside of this fire cool?"

40

ka zam tsi gǀae ǀ'u ha nǀai
and the turtle came and put his head

ka ko "hia he o hia hi n!ang...
and said "this fire's inside is...

42

te hi n!ang ǀoa khui te ǁ'un"
but its inside isn't hot but warm"

ka ko, "ee, hia he o hia goaq si
and said, "yes, this one is the one that long ago they

44

sa ǁama khuin to'a sa tsi tza khuin ke"
they two came from here and came and slept here"

ka siǃa ce ka to'a ka u ka u ka u ka u ka u ka u ka

46 *then they again went there and went and went and went and went and went and went and*

and

u ho yaa da'a nǀui
went and saw another fire

ehee

48 *yes*

ka ha u, ha u ǃhuia ha nǀai ko hi nǃang
then he went, he went and stuck his head into its center

ka ha ko, "nǁaq'aa,

50 *and he said, "(onomatop.),*

mi nǀai ku'u ǃai
my head is burning to death

mi cu"

52 *I'm going to lie down"*

ha zam koe nǁae ka ǃhuia cu ha nǀai ko ka kxa, ka sin ko "ee,
the turtle thus said and squeezed down his head against the ground and just said "aha,

koa ke re sa goaq‡'an tza?"

54 *did they sleep here yesterday?"*

ha koe se kxui
he thus looked around

ka ǃoa siǃa ka ka

56 *and told them that*

ka ǀoe gǀae cu ka u
they should just go together

ǀoe ku ko ka ku ko

58 *just do thus and do thus*

ha ǁxam te ua ua ha nǃang nǀui
he went along and went went to the eland 's death place

te "yaa da'abi re gea kore?

60 *and "where are the children?*

mi mhsi haa ǃXuma sa Khaǁ'an re gea kore?
where are my children ǃXuma and Khaǁ'an?

(okaa ha za'a se he ǃ'han)

62 *(it was that he had already seen and knew)*

"haa ǃXuma sa Khaǁ'an re gea kore?"
"where are ǃXuma and Khaǁ'an?"

"e sa ǀoa ǃ'han ǃXuma sa Khaǁ'an"

64 *"we are those who don't know ǃXuma and Khaǁ'an"*

ha tsi gǀae se te se te se tama
he came and looked and looked and didn't find

66 ǁ'akaa ha kua
and then he quickly

ha, hatce re a te !'han tcisa ke o g!kauce he ku ko "tcaqu,kaquu,kaquu"?
he, what is, you know those things that are pied babblers (birds) here that say "(ono-matop.)"?

68 ee
yes

ǁ'akaa ha
so that he

70 kua nǀhui ǁ'akaa sa te ko, " tcaq'aba, baq'a,baq'a, baq'a"
quickly took those things that said "(onomatop.)"

te tci nǀui ǀoa hui si
but nothing helped them

72 te ha nǀhui ǁ'a si sa te gǀae n!o'an u
and he took those things and went and threw them away

n!o'an u
threw them away

74 te ko
and said

"mi,mi mhisi re mi ca ku ho?
"my, my children will I ever see?

76 ka ke hi kuriha ǁoeh !ao..."
that they long ago thus died..."

ee
yes

78 te ǁ'akaa ha
and then he

ha ku gu ha he ka n‡ai djxania ha
he took this one and made him dance

80 ka ha mhisi ǀoa g!a'i
but his children didn't come out

ka ha gu ha he, ka n‡ai djxania ha
and he took this one, and made him dance

82 ee, ka ha mhisi
yes, but his children

ǀoa g!a'i, ka ha gu ha he ka n‡ai djxania ka ha mhisi ǀoa g!a'i
didn't come out, so he took this one and made him dance but his children didn't come out

84 te ha tsi gǀae
and he came

du yaa, du yaa da'a ku ǁ'ua nǀa'an
did the, did the fire that hangs in the sky

86
he hi hin to'a he ku !hun ju
this fire here that kills people

mi he
I here

88
ǁ'akaa ha du ha
then he did it

ee
yes

90
ǂaeha ka tci n!a'an nǀa te ju ka...
went to that big thing there of course and people were...

"ǀaqin-ǀaqin-ǀaqin-ǀaqi-ǀaqin
"(onomatop.)

92
ǀaqan-ǀaqan, taa tia khuian
(onomatop.), I'm like this

ǀaqan-ǀaqan, taa tia khuian
(onomatop.), I'm like this

94
ǀaqa-ǀaqa, taa tia khuian"
(onomatop.), I'm like this'

aie
mother

96
te yaa da'a
and the fire

yaa da'a khaua te ǁ'a nǀuia hin to'a ha ko
the fire (meteor) came down at the death-place (of the eland) there and he said

98
"ho koh"
(expression of excitement\aggression)

te nǂa'm gǂhu
and (it) knocked-smeared

100
te ha ko "ǀaqe
and he said "(onomatop.)

ǀaqe ǀaqe
(onomatop.)

102
g!aq'i tzau ǀ'hain ǀ'hain ǀ'hau
(lisping nonsense speech of the god)

ǀ'hainǀ'hain ǀ'aoro" ka ha ko ha mhsi g!a'i
(more lisping speech) and that's how he said his two children should come out

104
te ha da'aabi, ha !Xuma sa Khaǁ'an khu g!a'i
and his children, !Xuma and Khaǁ'an jumped out

ee
yes

106
te ha tah ko "ǀ'hain
and he himself said "(onomatop.)

‖'a tcia khoe
so things are like that

108 itsa m, !Xuma sa Kha‖'an,
you two, !Xuma and Kha‖'an,

|oa g!a'i n|ang
(why) don't you come out so that

110 e!a u n|hui !ha u te ku du
(lisping) (why) don't we take the meat and leave and do

‖'a ju te g!a'i te
then the people came out and

112 ‖'a kahin si n|hui !ha te
then they took the meat and

ka ‖au n|ang te 'm !ha te ju n|oa
they sat well and ate meat and people cooked

114 !ha te ha 'm te 'm te
meat and he ate and ate and

si n|hui !ha te ‖'a si te g|ae u
they took the meat and then they went off

116 n‡au u ka tju|ho
went home to their village

ee
yes

118 tcisa ju !ae n‖aahn n‖ae
things that the old people long ago told

hajuin mi hin koh tsa'a?
from whom did I here hear it?

120 tci !ae |'hoansi
true old things

Chapter 13

The Haregirl and the Moon

SUMMARY. When the animals were still people, their old man, Moon, one day went down into a hole in the ground. The people thought he had died, and wondered who would take care of them. They drank water from their waterhole and moved on to another waterhole when the water died. Later the raisin berries were ripening in their abandoned village, so the women were going back there to collect it and were bringing it home to the new village. One day one of their women, the haregirl, went with them to the raisin berry patch. The other women deceived her about which ones to gather, saying she should eat the red ones, and only gather the white ones. She did so, and when she opened her carrying skin they scolded her for collecting unripe berries. They told her to dump those out and go back for ripe ones– that they would wait for her. She did so, and while she was gone, they all pissed in the waterhole and told the piss to answer when she called out, so that the haregirl would think the other women were still there. When she came back to the abandoned village with her second batch of gathered berries and other things, she was eating a !ama bulb. She didn't see the women, so she called out and the piss answered.

Meanwhile, the old man Moon had found a tortoise and was sitting at the entrance to his hole in the ground at the abandoned village. He tried to entice the haregirl to give her the !ama bulb, but she was afraid because she thought he was a dead person. She stuck the bulb on the end of her digging stick so she wouldn't have to come close to him, but he grabbed the stick and pulled her into the hole. Moon said, "Why are you afraid of me? I'm still alive, and I want to give you a message so you can tell the other people. Tell them that when people die they will imitate me, the Moon, and will be alive again." The haregirl ran back to her people and told them, "Old Moon says that when people die they will not return, that their flesh will smell

59

bad." She then returned to Moon and told him what she had said to the people. He was angry and split her mouth with an axe; that's why the hare has a split mouth. She then took her gemsbok skin cloak and charred it in the fire. When she threw it over the Moon's face, the dirt of the female gemsbok skin made the marks on his face that we see today.

SPEAKER.   *!Unn|obe Morethlwa*

RECORDED.   Kauri, Botswana, 1971

TRANSCRIBED BY. *Tsamkxao Fanni |Ui, Jafet Gcao Nqeni, |Ai!ae Fridrick |Kunta*

ehee
yes
ju gesin sa o
2
some people who were
||'a !hamhi sa tsi ||a'ike n|a g‡hahan o ju|'hoansi te !xuni
those little animals of today long ago were people and lived
te ha n!ui n!a'an ha hin tsi he ku n!un, kohm, ku se ||'a o si o Ju|'hoan te si !xuni
4
and the old moon here was standing, and saw that they they were Ju|'hoansi and were living
te ||'atca tsi ke ha ka ku
and then at that time he
g!a'ama ka n!un n!un ka m ko ha te !ai ka ha g|a'i ||'atca hin tsi ha o
6
entered (went down) and stayed stayed so we said he died and then came out, that is what he did
si ku !xuni oo te ha !ai
they went on living and he died
te si ko "huu, n!au n!a'an o e ma ka !ai
8
and they said "huu, our old man has died
hajoe xae ka ku !om-!om e te n!aua he !ai?"
who will keep us healthy if this old man has died?"
si koe n||ae te !xuni te !xuni te !xuni te kua tsi !au
10
they thus said and lived and lived and lived and soon left
te u
and went
te g!u n!ang ma si koh ku tchi khoe n!un te si koh !xoana koa ke te ha !ai te si
12
and the little water hole they were drinking from thus stood and they lived over here and he died and they
!au !hara ||'a g!u n!ang ma te g|ae !xoana koa ke
moved across that little waterhole and went and lived over here

te nǀang nǃoma ǁ'a ǁaunǀhoa o si ga
14 *and the raisin berries had ripened in their abandoned village*

nǀang nǃoma te si
the raisin berries had ripened and they

si ku ǁama ǁ'akoa te ku !'hu ka
16 *they came from there and were gathering it*

te ku tsi gǁaan ka khau ka khau ka khau ka ku tani ka, te ku
and went and spent the day and collected and collected and collected and were bringing it home, and

si !'hu ka khau ka, ka tani ka
18 *they went gathering and picked it and brought it home*

te ǁa'i nǀui he oo si!a !'hu ka te
and one day they all gathered it and

ǁ'a dshaua hin o !'hai
20 *that woman who was a hare*

ǁ'a !'hai hin tsi o !'hai ma tze
that hare was a small hare

ǁ'a ha o, ǁ'a dshaua o dshau ǀ'hoan di te ge ǀxoa si!a
22 *and she was, that woman was a regular woman who stayed with them*

si!a !'hu ka te
they gathered it and

u g!a'ama ka ǀho te si!a !oa ha, si!a gesin tcoahn ha
24 *went and entered the raisin berry patch and they all told her, some of them deceived her*

te ko, "otca e!a hin ku 'm nǀang sa
and said, "we here are eating raisin berries that are

g!aan te ku khau ka sa !a'u
26 *red and are picking those that are white*

nǀang a hin ǁ'a tci-tcia a oo khaua, nǀang nǁah ǁ'a a khau ǀ'u nǀang sa g!aan
now you should gather the same way, don't gather and put (in the bag) those that are red

ka si tcoahn ha
28 *that's how they deceived her*

te ha re ku gom ǁ'atca te khau ka tzanasi te gom ǁ'atca te khau ka tzanasi te
and did she swallow those and pick the unripe ones, and swallow that and pick the unripe ones and

si !'oansi g!a'in
30 *their carrying skins were full*

te si ka ku, si sin tani ka te kharu ǁ'a g!u-nǀang ma te g!hoo
and they, they just brought them and went down to the little waterhole and sat

te si ko "!'hai, a koara tci !'an o a ga nǀang e se"
32 *and they said "hare, take off your carrying skin so we can see"*

te si kua si koara ka te ka !xau te o tci tzanasi re
and they quickly, they took it off and were surprised that it (contained) unripe things

34 te si!a ko
and they said

"a he xae ‖oeh ‖au ku khau te e!a hin ku khau tci dore sin?"
have you in fact collected well and we all here have collected bad things?

36 te koara te ka
and took it off and it was

g!a'an te ha ko "g!omsi !a'u !a'u !a'u
red and she said, "white, white, white (diseased) crotches

38 hatce re i!a koe du ǀ'an mi?"
what have you all done to me?"

te si ko "ha-m taqm ka nǀang ‖'a a te
and they said "dump it out and then you should

40 n!uan ce, e!a te g!hooa koa tsi ke, te !an a
go back, we will sit here, and wait for you

nǀang a gǀae khau ka nǀang tsi nǀang m u"
now you go pick it and then come so we can go"

42 te ha taqm ka te
and she dumped it out and

!'hu u ka
went off gathering and

te si ko "otca m!a ku u,
44 *and they said, "we're going to go,*

ǀoa ku g!hoo !an ha ko koa ke te ku u,
we're not going to sit and wait for her here but are going to go,

nǀang i!a gǀxam
46 *now you all piss*

nǀang !oa gǀxama o i!a ga nǀang ko ka ha du he ku !'au
and tell your piss that when she calls out

‖'a gǀxama ku !'au ha"
48 *the piss should call to her"*

si!a nǀuia ku zi ku !oa zi ka ko "nǀa a du !'au ha"
(also) one of them shat and told the shit, saying, "now you call out to her"

ka si!a to'a ka u
50 *and then they went off*

te ha u
and she went

‖ama ‖'akoa te u khau, khau,khau ka te ku tsi
52 *came from there and went picking, picked and picked it and came back*

te gu g!xa !ama nǀa'an to'a te
and took out that big bulb (Ceropegia multiflora tentaculata) and

ku nǀoqn ka tsi
54 *was eating it as she came back*

te ku ‡ae-‡ae si kokxuisi te |oa tsa'a te ku !'au
and was listening for their speech but didn't hear them and called out

56 ka zi hin tsi !'au ka ha tsi g|ae se tama
the shit there called out and she came there but didn't see (the people)

ka ku !'au ka g|xam hin tsi !'au ka ha tsi g|ae se tama
so she called out, and the piss there called back so she went there and didn't see them

58 ku koh te ha n!au n!a'an
while she was doing that, the old man

ho a kore ko ||o'a te ||'a ha te n|anga ||'a tsii si goaq !om ha ||'akaa n|anga
had found somewhere a tortoise and then he sat at the entrance to the hole where they had earlier buried him

60 du cao ka tzi te n|ang te ||ohm ka
widening its entrance and sitting and chopping it

||ha ,||ha ,||ha ,||ha
(onomatop.)

62 te ha ko "hajoe xae ce te
and she said "who is this now again,

ju n|ui xae?"
is it a person?"

64 te kxoa ||'a jua
and looked for that person

kxoa ha te |xoa ho ha te o ‡aun te ha ko "yaih"
looked for him and didn't see him and was going past but he said "hey"

66 te ha mani te se
and she turned and saw

te ha ko "hoe"
and he said "come here"

68 te ha n!un mani te ku oo ||aea ||'a tca te
and she stood and turned around and was holding that (bulb) and

te ha ko "a m sin n‡haoh
and he said "you just walk

70 !'hae n|ang tsi na tca to'a a ku 'm
quickly and come give me that thing you're eating

!ama to'a a ||ae"
that (bulb) there you have"

72 te ha ko "ooh,
and she said "oh,

tca jua he tsi goaq !ai he oo !au, hajoe xae cete?"
that this person long ago died and left, who is this then again?"

74 n||ah te tsi, tsi n!uan tca
left and came, came and stood there

tjutzi khoe te n!uan koa ‡xan te !'anga ka ko !ai te
about as far as the house door is and stood far away and stuck it with a digging stick and

76
ku l'an ha ko ha te ha !xau te ko "'in-in
offered it to him but he refused and said "no

mi m |oa ooa a ko tci n|ui n|ang a tsi na
I won't do anything to you, so come and give me

78
!ama, hatce xae mi ku ooa a?"
the (bulb), what would I do to you?"

te a ku n!un ‡xan
but she stood far from him

80
okaa ju gesin ||ama koa ke te
and the other people came from here and

ku !au n‡au koa ke
and were moving here

82
te ha tse ka ku l'an ha !ama te ha
and she gave him the (bulb) and he

gu ha te ||hai l'ua ha ko dom n!ang
grabbed her and pulled her into the hole

84
te ko "a xae koaq mi?
and said "are you afraid of me?

a ko mi te goaq n‡au kore te ku koaq mi ,mi m
where are you saying I went that you fear me, I

86
ge te mi hin tsi he
am alive, and it is I here

te |oa dua a ko tci n|ui, te ku !oa a
and won't do anything to you, but am telling you

88
tsi !oa a ka a u !oa jusa, ju gesin sa u he
came to tell you so you can go tell people, those other people over there

te ‡aun, te !au n‡au koa ke
who passed by and moved over there

90
n|ang a
then you

bah ka mi ||koa a wa a ku...
but if I send you there can you do it

92
a ku du ||'atca?"
you, could you do that thing?"

te ha ko "inn, n|a"
then she said "yes, certainly"

94
te ha ko "!aah,
and he said "run,

!aah n|ang u, ua si khoea n|ang !oa si n|ang
run to those people, go near them, then tell them that

jua ku !ai
a person who dies

96

ha ku ǂoa mi ka ku |xoa
will imitate me and be alive

ka ku !ai ka ku |xoa, n||ah ||'a ha kua !ai, 'in-in
and will die and then be alive, he won't quickly die, no

98

n|ang ku !ai n|ang ku |xoa, n|ang ku !ai n|ang |xoa
he will die and then be alive, and will die and then be alive

||'atca ju oo
that's what people will do

100

oo |xoa n||ah ||'a ju ku kua !ai"
will be alive, won't quickly die"

te ha ko "inn, n|a"
and she said "yes, of course"

102

"a bah ||au tsa'a mi, u ||au !oa si?" "ee mi ||au tsa'a"
"do you understand me well, will you go tell them well?" "Yes, I understand well"

ka ha !aah, !aah,!aah, !aah
and she ran, ran, ran, ran

104

tsi g|ae si ku koe tju sa ke g!hoo he o ha gea khoe sa ke te
came and they were as close as these houses standing here, she was there and

!'au si te si g||a
called them and they stood

106

te ha taa ko "n!ui n!a'an o ha ku ko i
and she said "the old moon said you

ka i ku !ao i oo i
when you die you will, you

108

kua !ao u n|ang n||ah |xoa
will quickly die and be gone and not be alive

Ju|'hoan !uisi te ||ku |kau"
dead people's flesh will smell bad "

110

"!'hai m he tzin, n|a..."
"it is the hare coming along here, of course..."

te si ko "ooh,
and they said "oh,

112

a he bah xae ||ama kore te a kokxuisi koe ta'm?"
where has this one come from with speech that sounds like this?"

te ha ko "tca n!ui n!a'an koh !oa mi, kohm, mi ku !oa i!a"
and she said "what the old moon told me, for sure, is what I'm telling you"

114

te ko "i kua !ao n||ah ||'a i ku |xoa"
and said "you're going to die, now don't be alive"

n!uan ce
went back

116

te si ko "a nǀa ni to'a a te ko
and they said "you obviously should go away since you said

tsi n‡oahn e ko ka, nǀang a ni to'a"
came and told us that, now you go away"

118

te ha gǀaea ha
and she went back to him

te ku are ka ha nǃuan tzi he ǃoa ha ko ka ha gǀae u, te ha ko "tsi,
and wanted to stay outside and tell him that she had gone, but he said, "come,

120

tci nǀui a ǃoa mi"
you'll tell me something"

sa gǃa'ama te tsi gǀae
they two went in and arrived

122

"a bah u koh hatce ǃoa kxui si?"
"what did you go and tell them?"

"mi nǀa koh ko si
"I certainly said they

124

ǃao u nǀang ǁ'a si te oo,
would die and go away , that's how it would be,

juǀ'hoan ǃuisi te ǁku ǀkau"
that dead people's flesh will smell bad"

126

te ha kua tsi
and he quickly

gu ǀ'ai te ka ǁohm ǃhara ha tzi, ka to'a, ǀ'hai tzi ka khoe
took an axe and chopped-split her mouth, that is why the hare's mouth is like that

128

te gǃo'e ǃ'an ha ko ǃoq'u he o ha ku tsi
and the gemsbok skin she had wrapped around her she quickly

gǃxa, ha he o ǀ'hai te
took it off, this one who was the hare and

130

gǁxuan da'a te tse
lay it on the fire and

nǁoba kxai ha
threw it over

132

ǀ'hoan ǀho, ka tsi ka to'a ka
the man's face, and that's why the

nǃui ǀho koh
moon's face

134

o ǀkurisi
is dirty

tsi o ha gǃo'e te ka ha ku
it was the gemsbok skin and when she

136

ǁua ha ǀho ko ka he oo ku ǃaah gǀa'i , ha ǀ'hoan ku
put it on his face and ran away, the man

138 koh ka g!o'e di ka Ikurisi ce to'a te koh xa gea ha Iho
since that time the dirt of the female gemsbok skin has been on his face

Il'atca sa l'u te dua Il'akoa
that is what they stayed and did there

140 te Il'a !aia tsi ke te e ka kua ku !ao u te Ioa Ixoa
and that's the death here that we quickly die and are not alive

ka n!uan koa to'a
it ends here

142

Chapter 14

The Beautiful Elephant Girl

SUMMARY. The elephant girl's husband's younger brother was still in his mother's stomach when his older brother married the elephant girl. After the marriage, the elephant girl's husband brought her to his mother's village to live, and she gave birth to a daughter there. But there were no elderly people living at that village, so the elephant girl and her husband planned to visit his older relatives at other villages to ask for gifts for the child. The elephant girl planned to leave her daughter with a woman there while she and her husband went visiting. The night before they were to leave, the elephant girl and her husband slept at his mother's village.

The mother's stomach grew, and she was about to give birth. In the morning, her older son, the elephant girl's husband, was packing to leave. His mother was grinding ochre and rubbing her stomach with it. Her newborn son jumped straight up out of her stomach, saying, "Mother, rub your hands on my head so that I can go with my older brother." Everyone was astonished, but one of them said, "This is a sky's thing, so just do what he says: let him go on the journey with his older brother." So his mother rubbed him with ochre and fat and he left with his older brother.

At one of the villages of the old people, the husband was requested to bring his daughter so they could see her. He agreed, and they were walking to fetch the child at the other village. As they were walking past an anthill, the younger brother stepped on a thorn and cried, "Ouch, ouch, ouch!" Then he took off his shoes and threw them away, saying they should go off and become vultures that drop down on meat. Then the younger brother said, "Run, older brother, go see what those vultures are dropping on, and get meat for us to eat."

Meanwhile, the older brother's wife, the elephant girl, was wearing

69

a skin apron with a metal awl stuck in its waistband. The younger brother asked his brother's wife to use the awl to pull out the thorn from his foot. The elephant girl believed what he said and came close. He took the awl and killed her.

The elephant girl had already told her grandmother that she didn't trust her husband's younger brother. She had said, "My thoughts don't agree with a thing that jumps out of its mother's stomach saying it wants to accompany its older brother. So watch well: a little wind will come to you with droplets of my blood, and will stick to your groin. Take the bit of blood and put it into something like a little bowl or a jar." And indeed the little wind with the blood came to the grandmother and stuck to her. The grandmother said in her heart, "Isn't this just what the child said would happen?" She took the blood and put it in a jar, and lived and thought. She said to herself, "If they've already completed what she told me, there's nothing to be done."

Meanwhile, the elephant girl's brothers went to follow her husband and his younger brother, to see if they had arrived safely at the village with their sister. In fact, the older brother had gone off and had not found the vultures, and was returning to where his younger brother was. The younger brother had killed and skinned his older brother's wife, the elephant girl, and had roasted her and was cutting up and eating her fat. The older brother arrived and, not seeing his wife, asked what kind of meat it was. The younger brother told him not to ask so many questions, but just to come and taste the meat. "Why do you call that which is meat, a woman?" asked the younger brother.

The older brother was greatly upset and asked his younger brother how he would manage to remain alive if he ate a piece of his own wife. "Stick with me," said the younger brother, insisting again that it was plain meat. Finally the older brother took a piece and ate it. At that moment the brothers of the elephant girl, having tracked the two, were seen approaching. The younger brother told the anthill to break open so his brother could enter and avoid the anger that was coming his way. The anthill obeyed, and the older brother stepped inside. The anthill closed. The younger brother stood alone outside, and when the elephant girl's brothers tried to stab him, he perched on the points of their spears like the little bird called ǁomhaya. He dodged their spears, perching on their heads, perching on their noses, and perching on their other body parts, and eventually defeated them completely. They left him and went off.

The older brother jumped out of the anthill and the two of them took the meat and went home to their village. The people asked,

"What have you done with the woman whose child is standing over there? What kind of meat is that you are walking around with your stomachs full of? You two have done something very wrong."

Meanwhile the bit of blood stayed in the grandmother's jar and grew. The grandmother put it into a skin bag and it grew some more. It split the bag so she put it into something larger. It grew and split that too. Only the grandmother knew what she was doing and kept her intention, growing the blood into a regular big woman again. Finally the elephant girl was the size of a sack.

One day the women of that village said they would go gathering raisin berries, and they took the child along with them. The grandmother spent the day alone at the village. When the sun was getting low, she spread a reed mat in the shade and took out the elephant girl and set her on the mat. She ground ochre and spread it on her, fixed her and dressed her and hung her with ornaments, and fastened copper rings into her hair. She was the beautiful elephant girl again.

When the women were coming back from gathering, they heard the old woman speaking to someone, and that someone was laughing in response. The child asked, "Who is laughing in the village that sounds just like my dead mother?" The other women thought the child was crazy, but then the elephant girl laughed again and they all began to wonder. They arrived in the village and saw her sitting there. Her daughter cried, "It's my mother!" and dropped down and began to nurse. The other women asked, "Who has done this?" The elephant girl replied, "Granny, of course, Granny alone. The old people give you life."

Another day the two who had killed her came back to the village, and, seeing her, got a fright. But they still wanted to take the elephant girl to visit her in-laws. The grandmother secretly gave her a magical gemsbok horn and told her how to use it when she arrived at the in-laws' village. The elephant girl then left with her husband and his younger brother and they traveled a long distance. As they traveled, the elephant girl kept asking them to let her know before they arrived at the village. She asked about mountains, and riverbeds with water, and what the distance was between where they were and the village they would be visiting. Finally they passed a hill, then a valley of soft sand, and another hill, and came to a village beyond, where small children with clean tummies were playing around and laughing. The brothers told her this was the place.

The elephant girl told them to go ahead of her into the village, that she wanted to powder herself and then follow them in. When the two brothers had entered the village, she took out her magical gemsbok horn and blew on it, saying "These two brothers and their village shall be broken apart and ruined!" The horn blew down the village, flattened it to the ground. Then the beautiful elephant girl walked home.

SPEAKER.   !Unn|obe Morethlwa

RECORDED.   Kauri, Botswana, 1971

TRANSCRIBED BY.   *Tsamkxao Fanni |Ui, Hacky Kgami Gcao, |Ui Charlie N!aici, G‡kao Martin |Kaece*

‖'a !'hoan o !xodi ‖'a ha tshin
that man was the elephant girl's younger brother

ha !xodi ‖'aha !'hoan ‖'aha tshin
the elephant girl's husband's younger brother

² ee
yes

te-ee
and

⁴ te ha
and he

‖'a !arikxaoma koh
that adolescent

⁶ tsau,
he got up,

sa !'hoan ‖'a sa
with the husband, and they two

⁸ ‖ae sa mhsi, kohm, o sa hin
took their children, in fact, it was those two

te ka ha
and when he

¹⁰ ha !ari-
the adolescent (word cut off)

!'hoaan to'a ku gu dshauma
that man was marrying the girl

¹² he o !xodi oo, okaa
that was the elephant girl, that was when

‖'a !arikxaoma to'a ku n!o'o
that adolescent was hurrying

¹⁴

g!oehsi ooa koh–ha taqe koh sin kxae ha g!u
the shoes did thus–his mother just had him in her stomach

khoea ko ha
(was pregnant with him)

ha sin gea ha taqe g!u n!ang
he was just in his mother's stomach

te ha !o gu ‖'a dshaua
and his older brother married that woman

te g≠ara ha te gu ha te u |xoa
and asked for her and took her and went away with her

te u ge |xoa ha ko ha, ha tju|ho
and went and stayed with her in his, his village

te g|ae
and went

‖'akoa te gea ‖'akoa te gea ‖'akoa te
there and stayed there and stayed there and

te ‖'akoa hin tsi ha
and there at that place she

g‖a'ia da'ama ko ‖'akoa
gave birth to a child there

da'ama o dshauma
the child was a girl

te ha koe te ha
and she was this big and she

ka n‖ah ha
left her

dshau ku se da'ama
a woman was looking after the child

koa ju!ae sin koara
where there were no old people

ee, ha, ha |'uisi tju|ho hin tsi ha n!haeta gea
yes, she was already staying at her, her in-laws' village

ee, te te ‖ama ‖'akoa te
yes, and and from there and

te te
and and

g≠ara u ha ju !aesi
went to ask from his old people

te u ku g≠ara
and went and was asking

xaro tciasi, !oa ha ju !aesi ‖'a ha tsi
for gifts, telling his old people that he had arrived

n≠ai kxaea da'ama, n≠ai kxaea ha dshau

36   *so that he could cause his child to have things, cause his wife to have things (get gifts given to them)*

te ǁ'akaa ha dshau te gea ha ju !aesi tjuǀho te ha koe u te

and then his wife stayed at his old people's village and he went off this way and

g!a

38   *arrived back home*

te tza

and slept

te ha taqe

40   *and his mother's*

g!u !'am

stomach grew

te ha ku nǁuri ka ha ǁamm

42   *and she was about to give birth*

te ge

and stayed

te si

44   *and they*

ha tza te tsau te gǁaan te tza

he slept and got up and spent the day and slept

te ha khoma te ku abasi ǀ'an ka ha

46   *and in the morning he packed so that he*

ce

(could) go back

te ha taqe xai g!oq'in

48   *and his mother ground ochre*

g!oq'in

ochre

te ku nǁhom ha

50   *and rubbed her*

g!u

stomach

te hahin tse tsaua ha taqe g!u n!ang

52   *and he then jumped out of his mother's stomach*

te ha taqe du ha g!u, du ha g!u, du ha g!u te

and his mother did her stomach, did her stomach, did her stomach and

du ǁ'ai te ǀ'an ha !o

54   *made beads and gave (them to) his older brother*

te

and

ha ǁama khuin tsi ke te khu g|ai

56   *he came from there and jumped out*

‖ama khuin tsi ke te khu g‖ai te ko, "aia, ee"
came from there and jumped out and said, "mother, yes"

58 te ko, "aia, g‡hua a g!ausi ko mi n‖ai n‖ang mi
and said, "mother, rub your hands on my head so that I

u ǀxoa mi !o"
can go with my older brother."

si ko si tam te si nǀui !xau te ko, "tca o nǀa'an tcia, n‖ang iǀa sin tsi n‖aahn tam.
60 *they said they were surprised but one of them refused and said, "this is a sky's thing, so don't you all say you're surprised.*

n‖ang sin du tca ha hin ku n‖a
just do what he says

da'ama tcia ne m ǀoa ku khu g‖aia ju n‖ang ka ku kokxui te iǀa hin ku tam ka?
62 *what kind of child is this who jumps out of a person's stomach and talks and you here are surprised at it?*

sin du ha
just do him

n‖ang ha g‖ae u ua to'a he ha ko ha u ǀxoa ha !o"
64 *let him go on that journey he wants to go on with his older brother"*

si koe n‖ae
they said this

ee
66 *yes*

te ha n‖homa ha ko ‖'a g!oq'in, ‖'a nǀaia ha n‖homa ha ko ka
and she rubbed him with the ochre, the fat she rubbed him with

te ha !o ku ‖xoba te ha ‖xoba ǀxoa ha !o
68 *and his older brother left and he left with his older brother*

te sa u
and they went

te u u u te
70 *and went went went and*

ua tjuǀho
went to the village

te sin ua tjuǀho
72 *and just went to the village*

te u tza
and went and slept

te ha ju !aesi ko, "n‖ang a,
74 *and his old people said, "now,*

itsa u tza n‖ang khoma tsi ǀxoa ‖'a dshaua n‖ang e se da'ama
you two go back and sleep and in the morning come with that woman so we can see the child

ehee
76 *yes*

koe n‖ae
(they) thus said

78 te sa u te ha
and they two went and her

!'hoan ko, "ee, m ku tani tsi ka i tsi se ha.
husband said, "yes, we'll bring her so you can see her.

80 ha n∣a tia g‖a'i ha ∣'ae te tia ǂaun
indeed she was born and is growing up

te mi ku tani tsi ka i tsi se ha"
and I'm going to bring her so that you can see her"

82 te
and

ha koe n‖ae te sa u tza te ‖k ae te khoma te
he thus spoke and they two went and slept and then got together again in the morning and

84 tza te khoma te ‖xoba
slept and in the morning left

te ka ku nǂau u sa ju !aesi tju∣ho
and were going off to their old people's village

86 te tsi g∣ae ku nǂhaoa khoe n∣ui te ha
and came and were walking someplace and he

ko, "oo, ∣'u ∣'u ∣'u ∣'ua"
said, "oh, ouch, ouch, ouch, ouch"

88 g!u'i
the anthill

khuin ∣'ae tsi g!u'i oo n∣anga
this is how the anthill stood

90 te si!a tsi g∣ae ku ‖xam koa tsi ke te ha ko
and they came and were walking along here and he said

"∣'u ∣'u ∣' u (?)"
"ouch, ouch, ouch (last word unclear)"

92 te ka n‖han ku to'a te ha
and was just then going and he

n‖aahn ‖'akaa te ko
left that and said

94 ya
yes

te g!xa g!oah, g!xa g!oah
and took off his shoe(s), took off his shoe(s)

96 te n!o'an u
and threw them away

te ko
and said

hi u du te o dxuu
98
they should go off and become vultures

te sa koh o dxuu sa koh taqma
and they became vultures that dropped

!ha khoea
100
on meat

te ǁ'a g!oah
and that shoe

tse u gea ǁ'a koa te ku
102
then went and stayed there (in the sky) and then

taqm te ha ko, "ye, mi
dropped and he said "hey, my

!o, !aah, !aah, !aah, !aah,
104
older brother, run, run, run, run,

hatce m !'ang !hun mi? nǀang a !aah nǀang
what is piercing killing me? now you run and

dxuu sa to'a a se nǀang du !ha nǀang mtsa 'm
106
go look at those vultures and get meat for us two to eat

te ha !o
and his older brother

te ku !aah ǀ'an
108
ran after

ǁ'a, ǁ'a g!oahsa
those, those shoes

te
110
and

ka sa ku koh ooa
when they were doing this

ha !o ǁ'a ha dshau ǁaqma
112
his older brother's wife was wearing

gǀxaian koe
an awl like this

te g!ai nǀo te
114
and sewed a skin and

ka ǀ'u nǃang ka ǀ'ae ko ǁ'akoa
and put it up straight there

te ha ǁaqma ka te ka nǃuan ha
116
and she put it on and it (the awl) was stuck (in the waistband)

te khuin ǁ'a !anua to'a mi koh ǁae
and it was like that metal tool I was holding

te ka ha !o !aah he gǀae ku !aah u he oo ha ko...
118
and when his older brother went and ran off, he...

"mi te o coea ‖'an tzautzau to'a te ku !hun me, tzautzau, kohm, !hun mi.
(said) "I'm going to pull out that thorn there that is killing me, a thorn, for sure, is
killing me.

120

mi !o ‖'a ha dshau, ha m tsi g!xa mi ko !hua ke
my older brother's wife, pull out this thorn here"

!o ‖'a ha dshau ku gaqea tca ju n|ui ku n‖ae
older brother's wife believed what the other person said

122

te tsi g|ae
and came

te ku ko ha se ka
and she was trying to look at it

124

te ha ko, "ha m g|aia ka se n|ang ‖'a a te na g|xaian to'a n|ang mi,
and he said, "stop looking at it and just give me that awl there so I,

n|ang mi !oa a ko ka n|ang a g!xa ka"
so I can tell you about it so you can take it out"

126

te ha !o ‖'a ha dshau ‡hoe ka te
and his older brother's wife pulled it out and

|'an ha ko ka
gave it to him

128

te
and

te ha koe du
he thus did

130

koe koha koe |xoa |'an
and thus didn't give

g|xain te...!xau
the awl...refused

132

te si ku, ha txun ku se
and they were, his older brother's wife was looking at

‖'a g|xaian te ha
that awl and he

134

|'u g|xain ko koa ke
put the awl here

(stabbing sound)
(onomatop.)

136

te hahin, ‖' a dshaua, te o ‖'a tca ‖'a ka n|ui te ha ni !oa ha,
and this one, that woman, had done that before and had already told her,

ha txun
her grandmother

138

te ko, "tca ke o tcaa
and said, "this thing which

‖ama ka taqe n!ang he g|ai he ‖xam ka !o he tsi komm o tca mia he tam.
comes from its mother's stomach and jumps out and accompanies its older brother is a
thing which I don't understand.

140
mi ‡'angsi m |oa zaihn
my brains don't agree

n|ang a
now you

142
maq ma ku tsia a
a little wind will come to you

maq ma to'a ku tsia a, kohm,
that little wind that will come to you, in fact,

144
tci n|ui maq ma, kohm, ka kxae
the little wind will in fact have something

tca o |'angma ko tcia
something like a little bit of blood

146
te |'angma to'a kohm ku du ka tsi g|ae ‖ua a ko a n‖hai
and that little bit of blood will come and stick to you on your groin

n|ang a gu |'angma to'a
now you should take that little bit of blood

148
te |'ua tci n!ang
and put it into something

n‖aahn kokxui, n|ang sin gu ka n|ang |'ua tci n!ang
don't speak, just take it and put it into something

150
tca o xabama ‖'akaa n|a ka o |xanama"
something like a little bowl or a little jar"

ee
yes

152
ee
yes

te si!a ‖xoba te g|ae ku du ‖'atca
and they left and went to do that

154
te ‖'a maqma tsi !aah ua ha
and that little wind came running to his

!o ‖'aha txun
older brother's grandmother-in-law

156
ku oo te ‖'a |'angma kua tsi ‖u
was doing things and that little bit of blood came and stuck

te ha se te ko, "hatce da'amaa he, a ni !oa mi ko tca ku du?" te
and she saw it and said, "what is it that this child has already told me about things that
would happen?" and

158
tse koe n‖aea ha !ka khoea te koe gu ka
then thus said in her heart and thus took it

"ka m, ka m, mtsa sin ku ‖ama koake"
"and we, and we, we two will just go this way"

ka ha ko "m!a u ‖'an koa"
and she said "let's go over there"

160

eeeeeeeeeeeeeeeeeeeee
yes

ha n‖osi khoea ka ku tsi du
on her skin it came and did

162

ka khoe si te g‖ae gu ha ka ha
it was as if they went to get her and she

ku du ka ka ‖'ua ka ko ‖xana n!ang–
did it and put it in a jar–

164

tcisa to'a o Huwe, kohm, a hin ko ka dusi te n‖a'ng?
those things in the Huwe (god) stories of long ago, for sure, do you here say their doings were nice?

te ‖'akaa
and so

166

‖'aha ge te ku ǂ'ang te ko "hin,
then she lived and thought and said "hmm,

kaa ke mi !uma !oa mi he u he
that which my namesake told me and has now gone...

168

xabase si m anexa du toan tca ha koh !oaa mi te nǂoahn koara "
although if they've already completed what she told me, there's nothing to be done"

ha koe n‖ae te koe n‖ae
she said thus and said thus

170

te
and

ha g!aa !arikxaomh gesin sa o ‖'a dshauma ‖'aha tshin !ansin kesin !o !ansin
she went back, those other adolescents who were the girl's younger brpthers and her older brothers

172

te ko, "he, ju-he, i ya m ‖oo jusa he n‖ang se xore
and said, " hey, people, now go follow these people and see whether

si xae ‖au u, g!a'ama ‖xoa jua u he ko tju‖ho"
they are going well, and have entered the village with that person over there"

174

koe n‖ae
(they) thus said

okaa hahin ane
it was that he had already

176

g‖ae kxoa n‖hoo ‖'a dxuusa te ‖oa ho
gone and looked for those vultures and didn't see them

te ha hin aneha koe !hun te koe tcxo te
and he had already thus killed and thus skinned and

178

‖'a tci, n‖a'ng !'hae tca ku tsi
that thing, quickly when it was coming

180

ǀxoa da'a te ka ha ku'u te ku !xai tchi ‖'a nǀaia
started a fire and roasted her and were cutting up and drinking (eating) her fat

n!un te !xai tchi
stood and cut and ate

182

te da'ama tia n!uan koa to'a
and the child herself was standing there

te ka ha, bah, ha !o ku tsi he, oo
and when he, what, his older brother came, then

184

ha dshau
his wife

"dshaua o mi ma xae o kore?
"where is my wife?

186

te da'ama u he te o nǀe'e te n!un
and that the child over there is standing alone

te ha hin ǀ'u
and that this one has put

188

ǀ'u da'a n!a'an
put a lot of wood on the fire

koe te n!un te !xai tchi nǀai xae o kaa ne?"
like this and that he is standing and cutting and eating fat, is what?"

190

te tsi
and came

ku n≠haoa koake te ko, "hatce xae a hin du te ka dusi koe?
was walking there and said, "what have you here done and your doings are like this?

192

!ha tcia ne xae to'a?"
what kind of meat is that over there?"

te ha ko, "ham nǁaahn !ha tcia ne nǀang ‖'a a te tsi gu nǀang tshan.
and he said, "stop talking about what kind of meat it is, just come and take it and taste it.

194

!haa a hin kurike gu te gaqea !ha, ku gaqea dshau?"
meat you now take that you once called meat, and call it a woman?"

te ha ko "n!u n!a'an koh n!a'an"
and he said " you big penis glans" (insult)

196

ha, ha !xau:
he, he refused:

"a ba koe kuru te mi hin ku naun ǀxoa?
"how will I myself stay alive if you are doing thus?

198

a ba sin !hun mi, wa?
are you just killing me?

a re ǀxoa o jua gǀai-ǀ'an m taqe nǀang ko tca ke koe, ‖'ahaa tsi gǀae ku
aren't you a person who left our mother's stomach in such a way, that you have come to

koe kxuia |'an mi ko dshau?"
200
thus ruin my wife for me?"

ko, "ham gu !ha n|ang ||'a a te tshan
(but he) said, "now take the meat and taste

tca ka ta'ma
202
what it tastes like

!ha |'hoan, te kohm
plain meat, of course

|oa o Ju|'hoan !ha
204
it's not human meat

koe !oa kxui a, n|ang a, kohm, tsi gu te
I thus tell you, so you just come and take it and

||'akaa n|ang n||han !hun mi
206
and only then come and kill me

a xae
won't you

ca tshan ka ka n||han !hun mi?"
208
just taste it and only then kill me?"

si n|a o ||'a tcisa ||'a ka n|ui n|e'e
they certainly did one of those things

||'a ha !o tsi g|ae gu ka
210
then his older brother came and took it

te 'm ka te ka o !ha, oo
and ate it and it was meat

te ha ko, te ha ko, "te mtsa re ku |xoa ka?" ka ko
212
and he said, and he said, "but will we two remain alive (having done this)?" and said

te ha ko "hatce re ku !'oan mtsa? mtsa m
and he said, "what will kill us, we two

|oa ku !ao
214
will not die

mi hin !'han
I know

tci n|uia !'oan mtsa o ka koara
216
there is nothing that will kill us

n!anga mi khoea
stick with me

ee, mi hin khoea a n!anga"
218
yes, I'm the one to stick with"

!'hoan n|ang te tsau
the man sat down and then got up

te ha ko
220
and he said

te si kaqǀ'hoan ǁama ǁ'a !arikxaosa to'a te si txun !oa si te ko, "ǀoo ju."
and they had just come from those adolescents and their grandmother told them and said, "follow the people."

222 te si kaqǀ'hoan ǁam
and they had just followed

te ha o ǁ'a tcaa te
and he did that and

224 ane ha ho si te ko "si m u to'a cu te ku tsi"
had already seen them and said "there they are over there, coming toward us"

eee
yes

226 "nǀang a !an mi nǀang mi du ǀ'an a ko
"now wait for me and I'll do for you

tca mi ku du nǀang a se"
something I will do and you will see"

228 te ha ko: "xa m du ǀ'an mi ko ka mia he, kohm, koara tci nǀuia mi !'han nǀang xa m du ǁ'a tca.
and he said "now do it for me, I here for sure have nothing else that I know, so now you should do that.

te ǀoa ǂ'anga mi jusi tsi !om mi"
and I don't want my people to (have to) come and bury me"

230 ǁxoba te gǀae, gǀae !oa
left and went, went and told

ǁ'a g!u'ia te ko
that anthill and said

232 "g!u'ima, !hara, nǀang mi !o g!a'ama, nǀai te ku tsi.
"little anthill, break open, so my older brother can enter, a fight is coming.

nǀang mi o nǀe'e n!uan tzi"
let me stand alone outside"

234 mm
yes

te
and

236 ǁ'a g!u'ia koh
that anthill

tsharaa khoe
split in two

238 te ha !o g!a'ama
and his older brother entered

te ha ko "nǀa a ka, !'o, !'o a, !'o a tzi"
and he said "now you should close, close your, close your door."

240 ǁ'a g!u'ia nǀa ǁkaea khoe
that anthill certainly closed together

te ha n!un
and he stood

242
te si tsi te ku, te ha se si te |om
and they came and, and he watched them and was cutting (meat)

te si ku tsi
and they came

244
te ka ha tsi he n!un te o
and as this one stood there and was

m ||'a e !uia, ha hintsi he ||'a da'ama
eating and serving up our older sister , this one's child

246
okaa si tsi tsia, si tsi
then they came, they came

te ku tsi g|ae sin ku gu ha
and came and just took him

248
jua ku,
the person was,

||'a ||'a tzamama m ge
that, that little bird exists

250
he koh o ||'a Ju|'hoan ma m ge
and who was that little Ju|'hoan, exists

xare ka tsi ke ha ge
even now he exists

252
te ka mtsa koh o jusa ku oo n||ho
and if we two were people who were travelling

‡ha sa ke o Ghanzi ‡hasi
these roads that are Ghanzi (Botswana) roads

254
||'a ‡ha sa ke m ku g||a ku g!a
those roads we traveled (together, years ago) to get back there

||'a ‡aah sa to'a
(on) those large, flat areas over there

256
ka koh o ju te sa
it was people and the two of them

te oo koa khoe e ku m !xoa ke, !oaakhoe
and did like we're doing, eating this pot and talking together

258
mi, a m ku tsa'a te ||xoasi |oa !'han
I, you've heard of it but naturally don't know it

to'ma khuin to'a ka ku ko
near there it was

260
!'ang, !'ang, !'ang
(onomatop. bird sound)

mmm
yes

262
mm-mm-mm
yes

'in- hiin
(onomatop.bird sound

264
ka tzema ka ǁ'a te
it's little and then

te khu koe du, ǁ'a tzama ha hin tsi to'a
it thus does, that bird there

266
ham sin o ǁ'a jua
it was just that person

te ko
and (they) say

268
te si tse ko "ǁomhaya" ko ha
and they call it "ǁ'omhaya"

ǁ'a Juǀ'hoansi o e gesin
those others (Naro people) who are like us Juǀ'hoansi

270
mi, e!a hin, e ko
I, we all here, we say

ko "ǁ'omhaya"
say "ǁ'omhaya"

272
ǁ'ang ǁ'omhaya
(onomatop.) ǁ'omhaya

ǁ'omhaya
ǁ'omhaya

274
ǁ'om.....................ǁ', ǁ', ǁ', ǁ'
(onomatop.)

ǁ', ǁ', ǁ', ǁ'
onomatop.

276
eeeee
yes

ee
yes

278
ha nǀa ku ko ǁ'ang ǁ'ang ǁ'ang
he certainly says (onomatop.)

ǁ'om, ǁ'om
onomatop.

280
ǁ'om ka ǁ'aha te ku (unclear)
goes (onomatop.) and then he (unclear)

ǁ'a ha te ku khu koe g!a'ama ka ǁ'atca ha ka koe du
then he thus entered and that's what he did

282
te si tsi gǀae ku ǁ'an ha
and they came and were fighting him

te ha ku ǁua !uǃu gǀa'a
and he perched on the point of the knife

284 te ku ǁua si nǀaisi
and perched on their heads

te ǁua Juǀ'hoan koa tsi ke
and perched on a person's (body part)

286 te si g‡xari ha
and they brushed him off

ju tzun
a person's nose

288 si g‡xari ha
they brushed him off

ha sin ǁxae ha
he just dodged him

te
290 *and*

ko si te ku ǁ'an ha
said they would fight him

292 te sintsi gǁa, gǁa, gǁa, gǁa te tlhoboga
and they just (onomatop. stabbing sound) and left off in despair

te ko, "jua he ha ǀho kuriba mi ku ho ha ka !hun a?
and said, "where will I see this person's face so I can kill him?

294 te ǀoa... m u
and won't ...let's leave

ha nǀa koh taahn m
he has certainly defeated us

296 ee
yes

oo cu," ha gǃa koe nǁae
let's go lie down," he went back and thus said

298 te nǁaahn ha te, te gǀae sin u
and left him and and just went off

ee
yes

300 ǁ'akaa ha !xau te khu-gǀai
then he refused and jumped out (of the anthill)

ku gǀai te ha abasi ǁ'a !hasa te gu ǁ'a da'ama o si ma te
left and he packed up that meat and took that child of theirs and

302 to'a te gǃa
went off and went home

si tju-ǀho
(to) their village

304 te
and

te
and

306 se te ha ko "yao,
saw and he said "yow,

itsa re g|ae kxaea kore ko
where did you two go and put that

308 dshaua ha da'ama to'a?"
woman whose child is over there?"

te ko, "a-o,
and said, you,

dshaua to'a...
310 *that woman...*

ka !haa mi goaq du etsa 'm he n≠haoh g|a'in,
the meat that I fixed before for you two to eat here that you are now walking around with your stomachs full of,

dshau tci tcia ne koma gea koake?"
312 *what kind of woman could possibly be here?"*

"ha m n||aahn koe n||ae, n||aahn a txun, yao"
"don't say that, leave your grandmother alone, yow"

te ha ko "!ha kah ke te mi ||ae
314 *and he said "this is meat that I'm holding*

te dshau ha o Ju|'hoandi ne re to'a?
so what Ju|'hoan woman could it be?

te da'ama hintsi i koh kxoa hintsi te etsa tsi |xoa
316 *and this is the child you were looking for, that we two have come with*

n|ang i gu"
now you take her"

te ko
318 *and said*

tsi g|ae ko, "e-e, itsa m oo tca |kau, n|ang itsa...
came and said, "no, you two have done something bad, now let the two of you...

da'amaa to'a a !oa ha ua ju sa to'a
320 *tell that child to go to those people over there*

te mi ku tsa'a khui"
and I'm in pain (over what you've done)"

te |'u te n||a te
322 *and discussed and talked and*

||'aha da'amaa tse ua ||'an koa
that child then went over there

ko ha |'uisi khoea
324 *to her in-laws' place*

te si ko
and they...

326 te u ge te u ge te u ge te
and went and stayed and went and stayed and went and stayed and

ha ku !'am, gea ‖'a ǀxana nǃanga te !'am
it (the blood) grew, stayed in the little jar and grew

328 okaa ha ǀ'ua ha ko !au
then she put it in a skin bag

ka !'am ka
it grew and

330 du !hara ‖'a !aua ka ha ǀ'ua ha ko hatce
split that bag so she put it into something else

ka ha !'am ka du !hara ‖'a tca
and it grew and split that

332 ha hin o nǀe'e te !'han te du ka
she alone knew that she was doing that

te ju waqnsi tam
and everyone else did not know

334 xoana te kxae ‖'a dshaua te du ‖'a dshau nǃa'an toan
(she) managed to keep that woman and fix that woman so she was a regular big woman again

o nǀe'e te kxae ha
she alone kept her

336 kxae ‖'a ǂ'anga te ku nǂai ‖koaa te
kept that intention and worked with it and

ka ha ku !'am ka ha ku kxoni nǁhoo ha
and she grew and she kept on fixing her

338 te ha ku !'am te ha ku kxoni nǁhoo ha te ha ku !'am te ha ku kxoni nǁhoo ha
and she grew and she kept on fixing her, and she grew and she kept on fixing her

te ka ha !'am ‖kae he ka tsi o dshau, hela
and when she had completely grown and become a woman, finished,

340 tca tsi ǀhao khuian ha tse khoe
the size of a sack is what she became like

te si ‖a'i nǀui tza
and they one day slept

342 te khoma te tuih te
and got up in the morning and

yaa dshausi ko si te !'hu nǀang,
the women said they would gather raisin berries,

344 te ‖xoba te !'hu nǀang, te da'ama ko
would leave and go gathering raisin berries, and the child said

"mi ‖a'ike ku ‖xam ‖gaqǀgaq, se ka
"I today will accompany auntie, see it

346
ka 'm n‖ang"

and eat raisin berries"

te ha ko "ha to'a u

and she said, "go on and go

348
‖a'i n‖ui ku ‖oo si ka g‖ae," ha koe n‖ae te n‖ae

this one day you'll follow them and go," she said and said

te ha tsuma ‖'a ha taqe si waqnsi ‖kae‖kae te

and her nephew's mother, they all got together and

!'hu u te ha hin, ‖'a dshau n‖a'an o n‖e'e te g‖aan tju‖ho

350
went off gathering and that one, the old woman was the only one who spent the day at the village

mm

yes

352
g‖aan, g‖aan te ‖am koe te ha

spent the day, spent the day, and then the sun was like this (low) and she

gu ‡oah te khara !hari te

took a reed mat and spread it in the shade and

g!oa !harisi te

354
in the late afternoon shadows, and

gu g!xa ha te n!anga ha ko ‖'akoa te tsi

took her out and set her there and came and

xai g!oq'i n te ‖'u

356
ground ochre and put it on

te du kxoni ha te

and fixed her and

tsi ka ooa ka tsi ooa te

358
came and did it and came and did it

n‡ai ‖aqma ha te n‡ai ‖aqma ha te n‡ai kxae ha te n‡ai kxae ha te ‖'anga ha ko ka ‡kai te (unclear)

and dressed her and dressed her and gave her (ornaments) and gave her (ornaments) and fastened copper beads (into her hair) and (unclear)

te ‡ha u ‖'ang ha te du ha te du ha (unclear)

360
?? hung beads on her and fixed her and fixed her (unclear)

tca ‖'homa o n‡angdi, !xodi

a beautiful thing, a python woman, an elephant woman

!xodi

362
an elephant woman

ee-ee, mi ku kokxui tama

no, I spoke wrong

ha o !xodi, mm

364
she was an elephant woman, yes

ha n‡angdi hin tsi to'a te si!a ku !hun ka n‡ah !o!o !kaua zi tzi

the python woman was the one they killed and the buffalo thorn seed dried in her anus

366 si ko tca tsi o n≠angdi
they say that one was the python woman

te haa he o !xodi
but this one was the elephant woman

368 ee
yes

te si!a ku tsi g!a
and they all arrived

370 |am koe te si!a ku tsi g!a te
the sun was like this (low in the west) and they all arrived and

ha, ||'a dshau n!a'an ku n||ae
she, that old woman was speaking

ka ha ko, "≠hain, ≠hain, ≠haan-oo"
372 *and she said, "(onomatop.)"*

te ha da'ama tsa'a
and her child heard

te ko, "hajoe xae ku tshi ≠oa aie
374 *said, "who is laughing like my mother*

ko tju|ho?"
in the village?"

te ha g||aq ko, "hatce xae mi !ui !ai te da'amama ku di, xae?
376 *and her aunt said, "what is it that my older sister is dead and the little child is crazy?*

ee, m !ui-m ≠xanha !ai
yes, our older sister long ago died

n|ang a n||au ko ha te tshi kore ce"
378 *now don't say she's laughing someplace"*

te ha n|ui ko
and another one said

"hatce mi g||aq !ai te da'ama ku di, xae?"
380 *"what is it that my aunt died and the child is crazy?"*

te ku n≠hang g|ai te
and left there and

ha tse te tshi
382 *she laughed again*

te ko "ha taqmaa-e,
said "(exclamation),

hajoe n|haisi xae?
384 *whose laughter is this?*

tca ju ani koara tju|ho, ju waqnsi tse koe !'hu, oo.
that already nobody's at the village, since everyone then thus has gone gathering.

dshauma tcia ne xae to'a te ha n|haisi ta'ma sintsi o ha |'hoan?"
386 *what girl is that whose laughter sounds like that which is really hers?"*

kaa si ku tsi g!a he oo,
then when they arrived,

388 se nǀang ha
they saw her sitting there

te ha nǀang te
and she sat and

390 te ha, ǁ'a da'ama ko, "aie xa , aie, aie, aie"
and she, that child said, "it's my mother (crooning word), mother, mother, mother"

!aah te kua tsi n‡hao te ku mq'm ha
(she) ran and quickly came and dropped down and began to nurse

392 ha nǀa koh ku mq'm
she certainly began to nurse

tsi nǀang te mq'm
came and sat and nursed

394 te si ka ku se ha te ka tse ko, "yao,
and they watched and said, "hey,

hajoe xae koe koh?"
who has done this?"

396 "mama, nǀa
"granny, of course

mama gu tsau mi
granny lifted me up

398 mama hin tsi nǁae te mi tsau te nǀang
granny here spoke and I got up and sat

ka ka koh i nǀang, mi ku ǀoa he ka ge
if it had been only you, I wouldn't be alive here

400 te mama hin tsi
but granny here

‡xanha gu mi
long ago took me

402 te ǀ'u mi te mi ge
and put me (in a bag) and I'm alive

te
and

404 te tsi te ha...
and came and she...

ya ju !ae ku ǀxoa ǀ'an ju"
the old people give you life"

406 mm
yes

teeee
and

408 sa ǁa'i nǀui ce te tsi te tsi ho ha te da'aba ha
they two came again another day and came and saw her and got a fright from her

ǁ'a sa sa to'a he koh !hun ha
those two who had killed her

410 te si gesin ko si koh...
and the others said they would...

"haa itsa koh !hun xae o haa ne te haa he xae o ha tcia ne?" te
"the one you two killed is which one, and this one is which one?" and

412 ha dshau nǃa'an !xau
the old woman refused

te !xau he ko, " 'in'n nǁahn koe nǁae ,
and refused and said, "no, don't say that,

414 ham sin ǀ'an si ko ha
just give her to them

nǀang tsau gǀae kxoni ha
now get up and go get her ready

416 ha hin tsi ku gǀae kxoni si"
this one will go fix them"

te si ko, "mm, nǀa, a dshau nǀa, a nǀa ku sin gu ha"
and they said, "mm, yes, this is certainly your wife, you certainly shall just take her"

418 ha tsau te ha ku ko...
she got up and he said...

ǀ'u te zaihn ha te ǁ'a si te zaihn ha te
discussed and agreed with him and then they agreed with him and

420 sa hin tsi ǁkae te tza te
those two both went to sleep and

ǁ'akaa sa ku tuih he oo, ha kua tse ko, "otca mtsa ku n≠au mi tjuǀho
and then when they two had gotten up he quickly said, "we two are going to go to my village"

422 te ha ko, "ǁ'an jua m ku ko etsam ǁa'i nǀui ua tjuǀho"
and she said, "that person says we two will go this day to the village"

te si ko, "ee oo, itsa te u oo,
and they said, "yes, you two will go,

424 hatce ba o ≠o?"
what's wrong with that?"

te sa
and they two

426 ǁ'a dshau nǃa'an hin cete
that old woman there again

gǃxa tca ke he
pulled out this thing

428 ka re... koa tsi ke ka ku ha ge
is it... here that still exists

gea Juǀ'hoansi khoea
exists among Juǀ'hoansi

koa tsi ke o ka tsi, ka re o...?
here it is, is it....?

ǀUkxa Nǃa'an hin tsi a ku se te
Old ǀUkxa here you see and

hoanah ko du ǁ'a tca
he is able to do that

o gǃo'e ǃhua si ku du ka
with a gemsbok horn they do it,

ku dchun ka ka ka ko "aari, aari,
they blow it so it says "(onomatop.),

chaari"
(onomatop.)"

te koe nǁae, ǁ'a gǃoe ǃhua
and thus it speaks, that gemsbok horn

si ku ǃhai, ee
they will wait, yes

siǃa ǃ'han ka
they all know it

ka si du ka, si du ka, ka du ka o koa tsi
when they do it, they do it, and do it over

to'a ka ka ǃaihn
here so it sounds

ǁ'a tca
and then

"mi ku are tcaa ke, si ǀoa du ka he, tci gesin si o du, ǀoa du ka he"
"I want that, they don't do this, that they should do other things but not this"

ǁ'a tca
and then

ha kua tsi gǃxa te ǀ'an ha ǃuma
she quickly took (it) out and gave her granddaughter

te ko, " gu tca ke nǀang ǁ'a te gǃam
and said, "take this and then hide

ǃkau ka
it well

nǀang iǃa u
then you all go

nǀang kaa tsi to'a iǃa u u u he
then when you all have gone and gone and gone

u sao ǁkaea tjuǀho
gone and all gotten near the village

450
he tjuǀho to'm
and the village is close

a ǃoa sa nǀang ko, 'itsa gǃa'ama tjuǀho
you tell those two and say, 'you two go on into the village

452
mi te ku n‡au gǀa'atzi, ka
I'm going to go (euphemism for) piss, am going to

n‡au tzi ka nǁhan gǀa'ama, nǀang
go to the bush and only then enter, so

454
itsa to'a,' ha koe nǁae, 'nǀang itsa ku gǃa'ama'
you two go ahead,' she thus said, 'now you two will enter'

oo nǀang a dchuun ka
do so that you can blow it

456
nǀang ǁ'a tjuǀhoa ǃao toan
so that village will all die

nǀang a hin ce nǀang tsi gǃa
and then you can return and come here

458
ce nǀang tsi."
return and come back."

ha koe nǁae
she thus said

460
te ha abasi te abasi te ha n‡ai abasi ha te du kxoni ha
and she packed and packed and she (grandmother) helped her to pack and fixed her up

te du kxoni te du ha te ǁauhǁauh ha
and fixed her and did her and (decorated?) her

462
siǃa ǁxoba te gǀae u
they all left and went off

te ha ko, "da'ama tse taa ku ku ǃau ǀxoa e te a hin ku u."
and she said, " the child herself will stay with us and you will go."

464
te si zaihn
and they agreed

te ha ǁxoba te gǀae u
and she left and went off

466
ka si u u u he tjuǀho ka ku to'm he oo
when they had gone and gone and gone and the village was close,

nǀang ha ku tsitsa'a si
then she asked them

468
nǀang a ku tsitsa'a ko
then she asked where

nǃom ku cu
a mountain stood

470
te koa o ǃomm nǀang gǃu ku cu te ǃomm koe
and where there was a riverbed with water in it and how the river was

te ha ku, te ha !oa ha te ko "mia ku tsitsa'a itsa ko tcaa
and she said, and she told him, "I'm asking you two about how

ka ǁkaekusi khuian nǀang itsa ǁau ku !oa,
the space is between (here and the village), now you two say well,

472

nǁ a du n!omma cu,
mention where a hill lies,

cu he ka n≠oana tjuǀho oo ǁ'a n!omma hin
lies here and is like the hill of the village

474

tse a !ain nǀang n!uan ǁ'a n!omma khoe nǀang
and its farmroad, then stop at that hill, stop there

nǀang, nǀang du ǁ'a tca"
now, now do that (for me)"

476

mm
yes

te sa n≠haoh, n≠haoh, n≠haoh te ha ku n≠haoh tsitsa'a sa te sa ku !oa ha
*and they two walked, walked, walked and she walked asking them things and they told
her*

478

te ko
and said

'n!omma ke he m cu,
"this hill stands here,

480

te !u cu te n!omma ke cu te !u cu
*and a valley of soft sand lies here and this hilll stands here and this valley of soft sand
lies here*

te n!omma ke cu t e !u cu te n!omma tsi cu ǀoo
*and this hill stands here and this valley of soft sand lies here and this hill here stands
following*

482

ka tsi ka o tjuǀhoa hin tsi to'a, ka tjusi tsi, a hin tsi te u se"
this here is the village, its houses are coming, you yourself will come and go see it,

ka da'abi !oa sa hi g!usi gaq'u he oo ku !aah nǁhoo he ku kxui tshi o"
*and small children with clean tummies will be running around and playing and laugh-
ing"*

484

ka tjuǀhoa hin tsi ha sa koh nǁa te ha ko, "yaq"
(she asked if that was) the village here that they two had mentioned and he said "yes"

te gu te ǀ'u ǁ'akoa, ǁ'a okxuia
and took it and put it into her thoughts, that speech

486

ku n≠oahn sa te sa ce te tse !oa ha.
she went on talking to them and they two again told her things.

ka sin n≠haoh, n≠haoh ka ua khoe nǀui
and (they) just walked and walked and came to a different place

488

te ha ko, "kaa ke xae o kaa ne?"
and she said, " what is this (place)?"

"i'in, ka ku ha ǂxan, kohm."
"no, it's still far, in fact."

"ehee"
"I see"

490

g|ae nǂhaoh ua ka n|ui te…"kaa ke wa ?"
went and walked to another and…"is it this one?"

492

"i'in, kaa o ka dore"
"no, this is a different one

te nǂhaoh te ka si ua ǁ'a n!omma oo
and walked and when they got to that mountain

494

te ha cete, "te kaa ke?"
she again (said), "and this one?"

te ha ko, sa ko, "kaa tsi he o tju|ho ga, hin tsi"
and he said, they two said, "this one is the one of the village, here"

496

te a ku se te da'abi!oa tshi u te ha g||a te
and she watched and little children ran off laughing and she stood and

hi g!usi gaq'u te hi ku !aah n||hoo ka kui n||hoo
their tummies were clean and they ran around and played around

498

te ha ko, "yaq"
and she said, "yes"

te ko
and said

500

"ee, n|ang itsa g!a'ama,
"yes, now you two go on in,

mi ka, mi ka ku ǁkaun mi l'ae ka n||han g!a'ama."
I'm going to, I'm going to powder myself and only then enter."

502

te sa tse ku g!a'ama te ha
and they two then entered and she

g!xa ǁ'a tca te
took that thing out and

504

dchuun,
blew,

ko sa hin te ko ǁ'a jusa te si
said that these two here and said that those people and their

506

si tju|hosi te ku xai
their villages would be broken apart

te xai si te ǁ'a ha te
and (she) broke them apart and then she

508

nǂhaoh ce te.
walked back.

tcisa tsi he ha mama koh ku n||aeh m ku tsa, he
these are the things our grandmother told us and we listened

510

eee

yes

ee, ha !'han tshii to'a te m!a koh goaq

512 *(story ends. beyond here is ancillary info only,so not translated)*

Printed in the United States
By Bookmasters